ANIMAL
ALERT
ABANDONED

ANIMAL
ALERT

ABANDONED

Jenny Oldfield

Hodder
Children's
Books

a division of Hodder Headline plc

**Special thanks to David Brown and Margaret Marks of Leeds
RSPCA Animal Home and Clinic, and to Raj Duggal M.V.Sc.,
M.R.C.V.S. and Louise Kinvig B.V.M.S., M.R.C.V.S.**

Visit Jenny Oldfield's website at
www.testware.co.uk/jenny oldfield

Text copyright © 1997 Jenny Oldfield
Illustrations copyright © 1997 Trevor Parkin

First published in Great Britain in 1997
by Hodder Children's Books

British Library Cataloguing in Publication Data
A record for this book is available from the British Library

ISBN 0 340 68170 5

Typeset by Avon Dataset Ltd, Bidford-on-Avon, Warks

Printed and bound in Great Britain by
The Guernsey Press Co. Ltd, Guernsey, Channel Islands

Hodder and Stoughton
a division of Hodder Headline plc
338 Euston Road
London NW1 3BH

Foreword

Tess, my eight-year-old border collie, has been injured by a speeding car. I rush her to the vet's. The doors of the operating theatre swing open, a glimpse of bright lights and gleaming instrument, then, 'Don't worry, we'll do everything we can for her,' a kind nurse promises, shepherding me away . . .

Road traffic accidents, stray dogs, sad cases of cruelty and neglect: spend a day in any busy city surgery and watch the vets and nurses make their vital, split-second decisions. If, like me, you've ever owned or longed to own an animal, you'll admire as much as I do the work of these dedicated people. And you'll know from experience exactly what the owners in my *Animal Alert* stories are going through. Luckily for me, Tess came safely through her operation, but endings aren't always so happy . . .

Jenny Oldfield
19 March 1997

1

'How long has Vinny been with us?' Paul Grey asked his assistant vet, Liz Hutchins.

'Nearly six weeks. Steve found him on the Morningside Estate at the end of February.' Liz bent to stroke the greyhound and boxer cross. 'You nearly died of the cold out there, didn't you, boy?'

Carly stood nearby, watching the stray mongrel whip his thin tail to and fro. She'd chosen the name, Vinny, herself. He was a rough, tough dog with a vicious footballing tackle. His

1

short coat had dark stripes across the back like a sports shirt.

'And we haven't had any luck finding him a good home?' Carly's dad glanced along the row of kennels at Beech Hill Rescue Centre. At this time of year, during the Easter holidays, they were bursting at the seams with strays and cruelty cases brought in by their inspector, Steve Winter. From bull-terriers to Bostons, from Yorkshire terriers to Great Danes, the kennel corridor rang out with yaps and barks, whines and growls.

Liz shook her head. 'Everyone wants a sweet little dog they can take home and train,' she replied.

Carly knew that the Centre had no room even for one more abandoned dog. The puppies that people had mistakenly bought as Christmas presents were rapidly turning into full-grown nuisances that tore up sofas and soiled the carpets. As soon as that happened, the same owners who had cooed over their live toys came rushing to dump them at Beech Hill, asking the vets there to find new homes for their untrained 'monsters'.

But poor Vinny wasn't even a cute youngster. He was getting on; grey in the chops and bandy-legged, he was a strange, cross-looking creature with one white and one brown eye, and a tuft of hair that stood up on his head like a bad crew cut.

'The problem is, he's been cooped up in here too long.' Paul Grey frowned as Vinny whined and scratched at the concrete floor of his kennel. 'It's reaching the stage where it's cruel to keep him any longer.'

These were the words that Carly dreaded. She turned to stack clean blankets on the shelf, gritted her teeth and got on with her work.

'I agree,' Liz said thoughtfully. 'Julie Sutton, the animal behaviourist, was in the other day. She said he was showing signs of distress, serious disturbance. She thought we'd have to do some-thing pretty soon.'

Carly's dad sighed. 'That settles it, then. Much as I hate having to destroy an otherwise healthy animal . . .'

Carly let her hands drop to her sides. Vinny might not be cute, or a pedigree; he might have a rough side when he was out in the park and bothered by other dogs, but deep down he was soft as putty. He didn't *deserve* to die.

'Let's give him one last chance,' Paul Grey decided. 'If no one's offered him a home by tomorrow teatime, I think it's best to put him to sleep.'

The two vets moved on down the row, quietly discussing this dog and that. Two of the puppies in kennel seven had been offered good homes. That left three more, including the runt of the litter. The highly strung boxer in kennel five had settled in well. Steve had made out cruelty-case notes about the cuts and swellings on his ribs. The dog would have to stay at Beech Hill until the case came to court.

Carly lingered by Vinny's cage. They'd given him a day to live. She added up the number of hours in her head. Thirty-one between now and five o'clock tomorrow. Vinny stopped scratching at the floor and looked up at her. He knew something was wrong. 'Come on, then.' Carly unfastened the kennel door and slipped a chain around his neck. 'I'll take you for a walk.'

4

It was like granting a last wish to a man on death row – any final requests, anything to say? Vinny gave a sharp bark and trotted eagerly at her side, out past Bupinda working hard at the reception desk, through the revolving doors, into the carpark, and down the side of the Rescue Centre into Beech Hill Park.

'I wish I could have him at my house,' Hoody told her. He was hanging around the park as usual, minus a jacket despite the cold wind that cut across the wide open space of green slopes, dull grey pond and carefully marked football pitches. He wore a sweatshirt, jeans and trainers, which he scuffed against loose stones as they walked along the path. 'But we only live in a titchy flat, and our Zoe says Dean hates dogs.'

Hoody lived on Beacon Street with his sister and her boyfriend, Dean. These days he spent a fair bit of time helping Carly out with dog-walking and the occasional spectacular animal rescue. Only yesterday, he'd climbed on to an old garage roof and released a pigeon that had caught its leg in the broken slates.

Carly let Vinny off the lead. He shot across the empty football pitch like a brown bullet. 'I wish there was something I could do!'

'Like get your hands on the people who dumped him in the first place?'

She nodded. Vinny had been as thin as a skeleton when he'd been brought in – all his ribs showing, and quaking from fear and the cold. Now he was happy and well-fed and his stripy coat gleamed with health. Carly watched him sniff around the goalposts, then charge off into some bushes.

Hoody whistled him back, surprised when Vinny didn't show up again.

Carly grinned. 'And he's normally *so* obedient!' she joked.

So they ran after him, across the pitch and into the laurel bushes. They found Vinny scuffling around amongst empty Coke cans and crisp packets. When he saw Carly and Hoody, he tossed his head and charged straight at them, aiming between Hoody's skinny legs in one of his famous illegal tackles.

'Watch out!' Carly warned.

6

Too late. Vinny bowled Hoody over and charged on.

But Hoody wasn't the sort to take it lying down. He got up and brushed the mud from the seat of his jeans. Then he picked up a stick and whistled again. Vinny stopped and turned, saw the stick and came bouncing back, ready for the game. He crouched at Hoody's feet, waiting for the stick to be thrown.

'Gotcha!' Hoody was quick off the mark. He held on to the stick, flung himself forward instead and slipped his arms around Vinny's neck. The dog squirmed but Hoody held tight.

Quickly Carly got him on the lead. She stood up and pushed the heavy locks of dark, wavy hair from her face.

'When you say "obedient", I take it you mean this dog doesn't do a thing it's told?' Hoody joked, standing up and brushing himself down again.

'No, but he *is* very good-natured,' she protested. 'He may look a bit of a bruiser, but really he wouldn't harm a fly.' Vinny took charge and dragged her off towards the pond.

7

'No wonder no one wants him.' Hoody was grinning at her efforts to control him.

It made her remember the cold truth about Vinny, after the larking about. 'No, and tomorrow we'll have to put him down,' she confessed.

Hoody flashed her a look. He chewed his lip and frowned at Vinny, who had begun to attack a litter bin at the edge of the water. 'Not if I can help it!' he vowed, turning on his heel and loping off down the path without another word.

'This may *look* like chaos, but there's method in our madness,' Liz promised the worried owner who was handing over a pet guinea-pig. 'There's a strict order to this queue!'

When Carly got back to the Rescue Centre, panting on the end of Vinny's lead, the waiting area in reception was packed with patients queuing for morning surgery. Cats miaowed inside pet carriers, dogs lay under chairs and benches, a big white rabbit sat hunched inside his cage. Melanie, their veterinary nurse, took the long-haired guinea-pig and carried it through to a treatment room.

'Fluffy's going to be all right, isn't he?' the little boy asked.

Carly and Vinny followed Melanie, listening to Liz's careful explanation.

'We're not sure yet. But tell me, do you keep Fluffy inside the house, or out?'

'Inside,' the boy told her. 'On the windowsill near a radiator to keep him warm.'

'Then he may be suffering from the heat,' Liz told him. 'Guinea-pigs prefer to live outside in a shed now that spring's here. Fluffy has lots of nice thick fur to keep him warm, you know.'

Along the corridor behind reception, Carly unbolted Vinny's kennel and put him safely inside. He flopped down to rest. Then she went back to look at Fluffy. The long-haired, black-and-white creature sat puffing on the treatment table. 'He looks like a wig!' She smiled at the sight. 'Or a mobile hairbrush!'

Melanie sorted out his front end from his back end. 'Your fringe is all over your face,' she scolded. 'No wonder you're too hot, with all this hair all over the place.'

Liz bustled in from reception. 'Long-haired

Peruvian. The glamour boy of the guinea-pig world. This little chap needs shampooing, brushing and putting in curlers to make him look his best!'

'Seriously?' Carly managed to put the Vinny problem to the back of her mind, as she took a green plastic apron from its hook and tied it around her waist. She was at her happiest during the school holidays, helping out in the surgery, carrying pets in for treatment, cleaning cages, assisting in the prep room with anaesthetics.

'Yes. And they're prone to heat exhaustion. If the temperature in Fluffy's house is over twenty degrees, he could actually have a heart attack and die.' Liz picked him up in the palm of one hand to examine his eyes, nose and mouth.

'A cat carrier to reception, please!' Bupinda's voice announced over the intercom. It sounded urgent.

'I'll go,' Carly offered, leaving Fluffy in Liz's and Mel's capable hands.

She picked up a cage on the way and hurried through. A black-and-white tomcat was struggling to leave the surgery before he'd been seen by a vet. He clung to his owner's sweater with his sharp claws and arched his back, hissing fiercely at the well-behaved German shepherd who sat quietly by the door.

'Pop him in here,' Bupinda suggested, taking the cage from Carly in her unhurried, unflappable way. Soon they had the tom settled inside. The owner sat down in the queue, underneath the poster advertising dog-training sessions, and the waiting room returned to some sort of order.

That was until two phones on Bupinda's desk went at once. Three dogs barked, the tomcat hissed once more.

Bupinda reached for the nearest phone 'Hello, Beech Hill Rescue Centre . . . Yes, I've told Paul and Liz you'd like to come in and film.' She looked up as Steve Winter walked in through the revolving door. Steve went to answer the other phone.

He listened, then scribbled down a message. 'Right, I've got that. I'm on my way.'

' . . . Paul did promise he'd try and find time to ring you back,' Bupinda went, still on the other phone. 'But it might not be today. He's very busy.'

She frowned as she put the receiver back down. 'That was a TV company wanting to come and shoot some film for a local news programme. It's the *third* call they've made today.'

Steve tore the note he'd made from the pad and handed it to Carly. 'They must think we all secretly want to be film stars.' He winked at Bupinda. 'As if we don't have enough to do! Look, Carly, this is a routine job, but you could come out in the van with me if you want a break.'

She nodded and flew out of the door before him.

'I take it that's a "yes",' Steve said, laughing, as he followed Carly out.

Carly jumped into the van, slamming the door against the cold drizzly wind and strapping herself in. The van smelt of disinfectant, with a whiff of animals. It was the Centre's only rescue vehicle and always in high demand.

'Ready?' Steve turned on the engine and eased out of the carpark. 'The first thing we have to do is call in on a Miss Harmony Brown. She wants us to look after her guide dog while she goes into the eye hospital for some overnight treatment.'

'Great!' Carly's dark-brown eyes lit up. 'What's the dog called?'

Steve consulted a note-pad glued to his dashboard. 'Brandy,' he told her.

'A trained guide dog?' Carly looked forward to meeting the dog and to the busy day ahead. 'What breed is he, do you know?'

Steve pulled out into the traffic. 'He's a Labrador; as good as gold and, according to Social Services, absolutely devoted to Miss Brown!'

She gave a satisfied nod. 'What then?'

'After that, we have to sort out that phone call I just took. It was from Bill Brookes.'

'Great!' Something else to look forward to. Bill Brookes ran an excellent (for once) pet shop on the main road into town.

'He wants to give us some info about four Labrador pups he was offered for sale this morning. Bill reckons they were way too young to be taken from their mother. So he turned the chap down.'

'What'll the owner do with the pups now?' Carly was immediately afraid that something bad might happen to them.

Steve kept his eyes on the road as the busy traffic ground to a halt. 'That's just it,' he said. 'Bill says the old chap shoved all four of them back into an old shopping basket and stomped out . . .'

The car inched forward towards a set of red traffic lights. Carly's eyes narrowed. Four tiny, unwanted pups . . .

'That's why Bill thought we should be in on the case,' Steve said, sitting impatiently in the cloud of exhaust fumes. 'And I think so, too, don't you?'

2

Brandy lived in a neat semi-detached house near a busy set of traffic intersections called Fiveways. His owner, Harmony Brown, was a young woman dressed in a bright-orange sweater, with tiny, carefully plaited locks and a warm, wide smile. She was blind and lived alone. Brandy had become her eyes.

'I hate to part with him,' she told Carly, standing at the door to see them safely off. 'Even for a day. When I heard I had to stay in hospital overnight, I didn't know what to do. Social

Services suggested Beech Hill for him. That's how I came to get in touch.'

'Don't worry, he'll be fine,' Carly told her. Brandy sat on the doorstep in his white leather harness. He was a cream-coloured dog with a broad head and strong body. His thick tail wagged gently to and fro along the ground. 'We'll take good care of him.'

'I know you will.' Harmony stooped to stroke him. 'And it won't be for long, boy. I'll see you tomorrow night.'

'Come on, Brandy!' Steve Winter stood at the garden gate, waiting to put the dog in the back of the van. Cars and lorries whizzed by along the dual carriageway.

The dog sat quite still, tongue lolling as he looked up at his mistress's face.

'Go on, there's a good boy!' she said smartly.

Brandy got up and trotted to the gate. He turned, expecting Harmony to follow.

'Get in the van, boy!' She put on a brave face and explained to Carly why Brandy was confused. 'He never goes anywhere without me. He doesn't understand what's happening.'

'I'll make sure he settles in with us.' Once more Carly promised to look after him.

'Thanks.' The broad smile and brave face faltered.

'You'll be OK?'

'Yes, fine. An ambulance is calling for me in five minutes.' Harmony raised her head, listening to the sound of Steve closing the van door. There was a muffled bark from Brandy inside the van. 'Say goodbye to him for me,' she said quietly, before stepping back and closing the door.

Feeling sorry for them both, Carly went and climbed into the back of the van with the sad Labrador. Brandy whined and whimpered as they drove off.

'Now for Pampered Pets!' Steve announced. It was the name of Bill Brookes' busy, well-run shop. To get there they would have to drive a kilometre down the dual carriageway in one direction, until they could turn off then travel back in the right direction.

Back in the flow of cars and lorries, Steve grumbled about the traffic. 'It's chock-a-block right up to Fiveways. Nothing's moving!'

In the rear of the van, Carly sat with one arm around Brandy as they lurched forward, then braked. A heavy wagon roared, then ground to a halt. A car horn sounded.

'More traffic lights,' Steve reported grimly. 'Looks like roadworks up ahead.'

'It's OK, Brandy,' Carly said gently. The poor dog was trembling at the noise.

'The lights are on red. Just smell the exhaust fumes from that lorry.' Steve began to wind up the driver's window.

But the dog's sharp ears had caught another noise beyond the grind and rumble of the car engines. He gave a sharp bark and raised himself on to his feet. Another deep, throaty bark of warning, ears cocked, suddenly alert.

'Hang on a minute!' Carly leaned forward to stop Steve from closing the window. 'Can you hear something?'

'Yes, traffic din,' Steve muttered, his eye on the red light ahead.

'No, a kind of squeaking, from over there.' Carly pointed towards the grassy central reservation of the dual carriageway. There was a sloping bank covered in tired-looking daisies and dandelions, littered with cans, old newspapers, cardboard boxes. 'Brandy can hear it too!'

Steve wound down his window and leaned out. 'Yep, you're right. More of a crying noise.'

Now Carly squeezed forward and hung out of the open window. There was a definite high-pitched wailing sound coming from one of the crushed cardboard boxes scattered over the bank. For a second she thought it was her imagination, but Brandy barked out another warning, and she heard again the pitiful high cry for help. 'Kittens!' she breathed.

Steve nodded. 'Sounds like it. Hang on, the lights are changing to green!' Ahead of them, the traffic crawled forward.

'Good dog, Brandy, we've heard it!' Pulling back inside the van, Carly settled him down. 'We can't just leave them!' she pleaded, peering out of the small back window at the vanishing cardboard boxes.

'Right!' Steve looked in his overhead mirror, heard the car behind blare on his horn. 'OK, OK, give us a chance!'

'What's happening?' she demanded, glaring at the driver behind.

'He wants me to get a move on, Carly. I think I'll have to go ahead. Otherwise, we'll cause an almighty traffic jam.' Reluctantly he edged forward, then braked again. 'No, it's OK, the lights have gone back to red!'

'Right, I'm going to take a look!' She decided in a split second, opening the back door of the van as she spoke. She heard Steve warning her to take care and telling her that he would drive off the road on to the central reservation beyond the lights to wait for her. Then she dodged between the stationary cars and sprinted for the bank.

The smell of petrol and diesel fumes hit and almost choked her. A huge black crow perched on a nearby crash barrier flapped his wings and took flight. And Carly could still hear the tiny wailing noise; a mewing coming from a box shoved against the barrier. Her heart was in her mouth as she made her way towards it.

The traffic hummed and the wind blew a sheet of soggy newspaper against her leg. She stooped to listen more closely. She had to part the long grass and push aside the tall, wild daisies. The mewing was faint and desperate.

Carly lifted one corner of the lid. Kittens: more than one, cramped inside a cardboard box, crying up at her out of the darkness. She held her breath as gently she unfolded the lid and peered inside.

Three kittens and a mother cat. The kittens cried out with hunger, the mother lay sick and feeble. She hardly raised her head as daylight flooded in.

Carly felt her face flush with a blast of hot anger. *How could anyone do this?* The cat and kittens had been put in the box, brought here and dumped. Left to die, ditched without even so much as a backwards glance, thrown away like rubbish!

But if they'd wanted the cats to die, they would be disappointed. Carly was here now, and she would do her best to save them. Quickly she glanced up, beyond the temporary traffic lights, looking for Steve. There was the van, parked a hundred metres down the road. And there he was, opening his door and looking for her. She just had to get the kittens to the van.

Not as easy as it looked, she knew. For a start, they were slap in the middle of one of the busiest dual carriageways in the city. She would have to cope with cars, lorries and bikes. Secondly, Carly found that the cardboard box was damp from the drizzling rain. The bottom was soggy and she was afraid it wouldn't hold together once she picked it up. There was a strong risk that she might drop the cats.

But there was no time to run for the van and fetch a proper carrier. These kittens had to be rescued right away. The mother cat especially looked as if she was on her last legs. So Carly hooked both arms under the bottom of the box and lifted it. The bottom sagged, but held. Drawing another deep breath, she carried it towards the van.

'Were we right? Is it kittens?' Steve cried above the traffic noise.

Carly was trudging through the overgrown grass on the central reservation, past the traffic lights, aware that all the drivers were staring and wondering. She nodded. 'Three of them. And the mother cat, too! We've got to get them back to Beech Hill as quick as we can, Steve. They're in a bad way. I don't think they can last much longer!'

Forgetting everything else, they lifted the battered box into the back of the van, and signalled to join the crawling traffic. The crying of the kittens went on; a dreary, hopeless wail. Carly crouched over them, fending Brandy off and looking more closely at what they'd found.

The tiny kittens were only a few weeks old. Born to the same brown and black tortoiseshell mother, who now lay so sick and shivering in the sodden box, each kitten had a completely different colour and markings. One was jet-black, with huge yellow eyes. One was silver-grey and the third was a reddish-brown tortoiseshell like her mother. Jet, Diamond and Ruby, Carly decided. And the poor mother cat was Daisy, because of where she'd been found, abandoned amongst rubbish on a bank where daisies grew.

'Steve, we have to get a move on!' she pleaded from the back of the van. 'This cat's too sick to feed her kittens. They're starving!' At the Rescue

Centre they would be able to mix a formula food especially made for kittens and hand-feed them through a syringe. She glanced again at their open mouths as they begged for help.

'I'm going as fast as I can.' He signalled and moved from one lane into the next, trying to weave through yet another jam. 'You can thank Brandy back there that we found them at all,' he reminded her. 'If it hadn't been for him, we'd probably have driven straight past.'

Harmony Brown's guide dog must have sensed that he was being praised. He gave a pleased wag of his tail.

'How much longer?' Carly did her best to wrap each kitten in a clean towel from the stack which they kept in the van. It was vital to keep them warm. Then she turned her attention to Daisy.

'Five more minutes,' Steve answered. 'I'll ring the surgery and tell them we're on our way. He picked up the car phone and gave Bupinda the message, dodging off the main street to avoid the worst of the traffic up ahead. 'Can you tell what's wrong with the mother?' he asked.

Carly knew a fair bit about illnesses and

injuries to animals. She'd been brought up to it, ever since she'd come back from East Africa with her father after her mother had died. That had been when she was four years old. Since then she'd been at his side, watching how he worked quickly and calmly to diagnose the stream of cases brought into Beech Hill each day. She'd seen how he would lift the fur at the scruff of an animal's neck to judge its condition. She did this now for Daisy. The skin on the neck stayed ridged, instead of relaxing quickly back into place. 'Like I said, it looks bad,' she reported. 'She's dehydrated and very weak. I can hardly see her breathing.'

'OK, almost there.' Steve wound in and out of the sidestreets at the back of Beech Hill Park. Eventually they came on to the road of once-grand Victorian houses where the Rescue Centre stood. But a big furniture van backing out of a driveway suddenly blocked their way. Steve braked hard and they squealed to a halt.

Again Carly knew it was time to act. Telling Steve to grab hold of Brandy's collar, she opened the back door and jumped on to the road. Then she picked up the box, careful once more to hook her arms underneath the mangled cardboard base. It would be quicker to run with it, right up to the doors of the Centre, into reception. So she sped along the pavement, trying to keep the box steady, still hoping that she would be in time to save the cats.

The morning surgery session at Beech Hill was drawing to a close. A sprinkling of cars stood parked in the carpark, a few late patients sat quietly in the waiting room. A dog barked at Carly as she dashed through, and put the box down on the desk in reception.

'What is it?' Bupinda asked, surprised to see Carly back so soon.

She opened the box to show her. 'Call for Dad!' she pleaded, gasping for breath. 'It's an emergency!'

And soon Paul Grey came running through from a treatment room, his shirt-sleeves rolled back. 'What have you got – an RTA?'

Carly explained that the cats hadn't actually been involved in a traffic accident. 'We found them on the dual carriageway, but they haven't been run over, thank heavens. Someone dumped them!'

Her dad frowned as he took a look in the box. 'OK, let's deal with the mother first. She's the most urgent,' he decided.

Mel came through with a carrier, but Paul had already picked the cat out of the box and was carrying her gently in his hands. Daisy lay limp, her head drooping, her eyes half-closed. 'It's OK,' he said to the nurse. 'I'll take her straight through to the prep room like this.'

It was as bad as Carly had thought, then. She watched the door swing to behind her dad, then closed her eyes and gathered her breath. One or two curious onlookers had wandered across from the waiting area to look at the kittens. 'Poor little things!' Carly heard them say. 'Listen to them, they must be starving!' and, 'Who would do a thing like that?'

Then another voice broke in. 'Do you want the good news?' it said.

'Hoody!' Carly opened her eyes. He was always popping up from nowhere. Maybe he'd been in the waiting room and she'd been too busy to see him when she dashed in. Now he hovered at her shoulder, looking secretive, even excited. 'Not now,' she tried to explain. Daisy's case had been taken in hand by her dad, but there was still Ruby, Jet and Diamond to see to.

'Not even if it's about Vinny?' he persisted.

She hesitated. One of the kittens, Jet, cried and struggled free of his towel. 'Later, Hoody!' she pleaded. 'Wait here for a bit while I take these three into a treatment room and get Liz to look at them!'

But Hoody shrugged, then sulked. 'I'm not hanging around here like a spare part,' he protested, turning on his heel and heading for the door. 'I thought you were meant to care about Vinny!'

There was no time to argue. And now the phone was ringing, and Bupinda was picking it up and telling the same TV company that no, Paul Grey wasn't available at the moment, he was caught up in an emergency. Yes, she would pass on the message. '*Again!*' She sighed as she put down the phone and raised her eyebrows.

Hoody scowled and launched himself at the

revolving door, disappearing out into the drizzle and the wind.

It was Carly's turn to shrug and raise her eyebrows. 'If he comes back, ask him to wait.' She sighed. The sound of wailing kittens was too hard to bear. She picked up the box and took it anxiously into room number three.

3

Jet weighed hardly anything when Carly picked him up, ready to hand-feed him. He was a tiny scrap of black fur, light as a bird, practically skin and bone.

'These kittens haven't been properly fed for days,' Liz murmured, tending to Diamond, Jet's silver-grey sister. She and Carly had prepared three glass tubes full of milk, each with a rubber bulb on the end which would squeeze drops of liquid into the kittens' mouths.

'I wonder why not.' Carly concentrated on easing

Jet's tiny mouth open by pressing gently on the sides of his jaw. Then she slid the tiny dropper in. As soon as the first drop of milk landed on his tongue, he stopped squirming and gulped hard.

'Gently at first,' Liz warned. 'Don't let him be too greedy. It's either because they've deliberately been kept away from the mother, hoping to starve them to death, or it's because mum's been too ill to feed them.'

'Daisy's pretty sick,' Carly admitted.

'In that case, her milk probably dried up.'

'She's a pretty small cat as well.' She mopped Jet's mouth with a tissue and waited for him to swallow the first few drops of milk.

'This is probably her first litter, then, and she may well be too young to cope with three hungry youngsters, especially if she's not been well looked after herself.' Liz sighed as she put Diamond into a specially lined, clean pet carrier and picked Ruby up to feed her next. 'It's all too common, I'm afraid. Whoever owned the cat either couldn't afford to have her spayed so that she couldn't have kittens, or couldn't be bothered. The result? An unwanted litter and poor mum unable to care for them.'

'I hope Daisy's going to be OK,' Carly murmured. It was a relief to see the three kittens taking their first food, like a weight off her shoulders. But now she worried all over again about the mother.

'Paul will do everything he can.'

Still fairly new to the practice at Beech Hill, Liz had recently got through vet school and looked up to Carly's dad as the expert senior vet.

'That's good, Carly. Do you think he's had enough for now?'

Carly nodded. 'You should have heard them crying on the dual carriageway,' she said softly, tucking Jet up alongside Diamond. 'I think it was the saddest thing I've ever heard!'

'I know.' Liz held Ruby cupped in her warm hand. 'I know.' She shook her head and smiled kindly at Carly. 'It's enough to melt the hardest heart.'

'It's enough to make me punch whoever did it in the face!' Carly admitted. 'Send them to prison, don't feed *them* for a few days. See how *they* like it!'

'That's my girl!' Liz preferred the fighting spirit. 'Listen, now that these three are safely tucked up and we're all finished here, why don't you go and give your dad a hand? Then come back and tell me how you've got on.'

It was the suggestion Carly needed to take her mind off the anger she felt. But she headed for the operating theatre with her fingers crossed, fearful of what she might find. Daisy had been very, very ill, she knew, and her chances were slim.

She took an apron from the hook and pulled it over her head as she went through the prep room and swung through the theatre door. The lights over the operating theatre shone bright, the steel instrument tray gleamed, an oxygen mask hung from its plastic tube, swaying slightly.

Paul Grey stood with his back towards Carly, stooped over the table where Daisy lay. The cat had been quickly anaesthetised and prepped ready for surgery. A patch of fur on her side had been shaved and the cuts made. Now the vet had to investigate what was wrong.

Carly slid alongside Mel, who stood at the far

side of the table, but she said nothing. She was used to seeing operations, was never squeamish or felt faint.

Her dad knew it was her without glancing up or pausing as his gloved fingers probed and reached for fresh instruments. 'What we've got here are postnatal complications,' he explained. 'In other words, when this cat gave birth to her kittens, she was in such poor condition that it didn't go as smoothly as it should have. She's scarcely old enough to have kittens anyway.'

Liz had been right, Carly realised. 'What exactly is wrong?'

'She didn't manage to get rid of all the after-birth when the kittens were born, so part of it has stayed in the womb and turned septic. That's caused a serious infection that's travelled through the bloodstream. It's dried up her milk and given her a high fever. Her heart's been weakened, I'm afraid.'

Carly watched Mel take the oxygen mask and lower it gently over Daisy's mouth. The cat lay on her side, legs outstretched, connected by a tube to a drip feeding fluid into her veins. There wasn't a single flicker of movement. Eerie. If she hadn't known better, Carly would have said that the animal was already dead.

'We have to remove the septic material from the abdomen, since that's what's causing the damage. But I'm worried that she won't be strong enough to last through the operation.' He signalled for Mel to stop giving oxygen and asked for a boost of gas anaesthetic instead. He was working as quickly as he could, glancing up at the clock that ticked on the opposite wall.

The red second hand jerked forward. Each movement twisted another knot in Carly's already tangled nerves.

'I can't see her breathing,' Mel warned quietly.

Paul Grey's rapid hand movements stopped. He watched the cat's ribcage for signs of rising and falling as the lungs took in air. 'More oxygen,' he said.

Mel tried again with the mask. Paul listened with his stethoscope. 'No heartbeat.' His voice fell flat in the tense silence.

Carly urged them quietly to keep trying. *Don't give in! Don't let her die!*

They did everything they knew to drag Daisy back to life. But all their knowledge and experience made no difference. It was too late. The cat had been neglected for too long, then abandoned in a cardboard box in the terrifying city traffic. Now, in spite of all Carly's and her father's efforts to save her, she was dead.

4

It was lunchtime on a rainy Tuesday. Daisy was dead and her kittens' lives still hung by a thread. In the kennels Brandy was whining and pining for his mistress, while Vinny the stray had less than twenty-four hours to live.

'Not a good day, eh?' Paul Grey asked Carly. He sat at his office desk filling in forms while Carly perched on the windowsill gazing out at the tall beech trees just coming into leaf.

She sighed. 'Sometimes I wish we did a nice, simple job, like running a sweet shop.'

He looked up and grinned ruefully. 'Don't take things too much to heart.'

But it was too late to tell her this when Daisy was already dead. 'The trouble is, I can't believe that anyone could be so cruel . . .' She tailed off. How many times had she said and thought this? Yet what difference did it make?

'Concentrate on helping to make the kittens better,' Paul suggested. 'Liz tells me they've taken a feed and now they're sleeping. She's given them a shot of antibiotic in case they've picked up any infection from the mother. So you know the routine from now on: feeding by hand, little and often, keeping them warm and clean.'

Carly nodded. 'You should see them, Dad. One's black as soot. I've called him Jet. And there's a stripy brown-and-red one called Ruby, and a silvery one called Diamond.'

'Nice names.' He sifted through papers looking for the notes on the cruelty case in kennel number five. 'Look, instead of fidgeting around in here, why not take off with our new admission, the guide dog, for a few minutes, and get a breath of fresh air in the park?'

'I still don't know how anyone can just dump animals like rubbish . . .!' Carly was churned up, frowning, clenching her fists.

'Carly: walkies!' Paul Grey commanded.

She gave an exasperated sigh and jumped down from the sill. 'OK, OK. I've seen Hoody out there. I'll go and ask him if he wants to help me walk Brandy. No, on second thoughts, I'll rope him into coming and taking Vinny for a walk too!'

She was off, glad to be on the move, shouting for Hoody, joking and asking him, didn't he have a home to go to? And since he was doing nothing, why didn't he give poor Vinny a bit of exercise?

'Anyway, weren't you going to tell me some good news about Vinny?' she reminded him, after they'd fetched the dogs from the kennels and were back in reception, signing them out on their walk.

'Forget it.' He shrugged and turned down the corners of his mouth. 'It might not come to anything.'

By the look on his face, Carly knew not to press him. Hoody had thin features, with frown lines between his eyebrows. And his short, bristly haircut made you not want to mess with him. Yet he was soft on animals. A strange mixture.

' . . . Yes, I will get him to ring you,' Bupinda was promising someone over the phone. She held her hand over the mouthpiece and whispered, 'It's those TV people again! I can't seem to get rid of them!'

'Tell them we're too busy,' Carly whispered back, explaining the problem to Hoody as they put the two dogs on leads and took them off on their walk. 'I bet they just want to come in and film some cute puppies so people can look at them and go "Aah!" '

'What's wrong with that?' Hoody asked, as Vinny tugged on the lead, going the wrong way round lampposts, sniffing at everything in his path.

'It gives the wrong idea. Animals aren't cuddly toys. If you see sweet little pups on the telly, you think you want one, without stopping to think whether or not you can look after it properly, day in, day out, year after year.' Hoody had hit a sore spot with her. The memory of the kittens in the cardboard box was still much too strong. She began to tell him about it, getting all worked up again.

They reached the park and let Brandy and Vinny off their leads. The two dogs chased each other down the slope.

'So you don't know who left them there?' Hoody was gritting his teeth, frowning as he spoke.

'We've got no idea. All I know is they were terrified when I found them, and we were too late to save Daisy.'

'And you found them in a box? What sort of box?' Hoody picked up a hefty stick to tempt Vinny with. The mongrel dog came racing back. He barked and leaped up as if his legs were on springs.

'How do I know what sort of box? Just a box. A supermarket box.'

Hoody threw the stick and sent it soaring. 'Did it have writing on?'

'Yep. It was for baked beans.' What did it matter? Sometimes Hoody seemed to go off on the wrong track altogether.

'What brand?'

'I don't know . . .' said Carly, exasperated.

'Think, Carly. If you want to find out who did this, it could be important.'

'OK, OK, it wasn't a name brand. No, that's it, it was a Hillman's box.' Hillman's was the name of the local supermarket at the junction of Beech Hill and the main City Road. 'So what?'

'So, that means the owner's local. They didn't drive here from a long way off then dump the box. Either they shop at Hillman's, or else they picked up the box from the big stack they keep at the back of the supermarket, by the railway line.'

Carly nodded. 'I get it. But thousands of people shop there. It doesn't really get us much closer, does it?'

'Better than nothing,' he insisted. 'Anyway, I'll ask around if you like.' He made it sound casual, like a tiny favour.

Carly watched Vinny come haring back up the slope with the stick in his mouth. Brandy took things more slowly, content to tag along. She considered Hoody's offer. When he said, 'ask around', it probably meant a lot of hanging around the supermarket, asking other kids if they'd heard of anyone with a cat who'd just had kittens. He was the sort who was always picking up bits of information, keeping his ear to the ground. She would never have the time or patience to do it herself. She was grateful, but she knew she'd better not go over the top and scare him off.

'You can if you like,' she shrugged, trying to act more casual than Hoody himself.

'You got here at last!' Bill Brookes beamed from behind his counter at Pampered Pets. 'What kept you?'

Carly's spirits lifted the moment she and Steve walked into the shop. Cages lined the wall. Furry brown hamsters trod on and on inside their exercise wheels. Blue-and-white, green-and-yellow budgerigars tweaked at their feathers or pecked at their little round mirrors. 'Who's a cheeky boy?' one croaked in a old man's voice; 'Beauty, Beauty! Who's a cheeky boy?'

And then there were rabbits in the pet shop; dwarf rabbits, rex rabbits with velvety coats, and bluish-grey chinchillas. They twitched their noses or flicked their ears, thumping up and down inside their spacious hutches.

Carly loved the well-run shop. She loved the smell of dog meal and biscuits, the red cat-collars with price tags hanging from their hooks, the squashy, foam-rubber-filled cat baskets and tough brown plastic ones for dogs, the kitten scratching-posts and brightly coloured balls with bells inside for budgies.

'Beauty! Who's a cheeky boy? Poppety-poppety-poppety-pop!'

Steve went and leaned on the counter, ready for a chat with Bill. Carly thought they looked funny together. Where Steve was sturdy, Bill was thin as a rake. Steve had dark-brown hair, neatly parted, Bill was fair with wispy curls. He wore glasses without rims, and spoke so fast that you could hardly keep up. Steve, on the other hand, had a slow, deep voice, and would rather listen than talk.

'Lightweight frame, twenty-four gears.' Bill was proudly describing his new mountain bike. 'I had it specially built. It cost me a bomb.'

'Mountain biking sounds too much like hard work to me.' Steve pulled a note-pad out of his jacket pocket, ready to get down to business. 'About these four Labrador pups, Bill; you say the owner was trying to palm them off on you before they were ready to leave the mother?'

'That's right. They couldn't have been more than four weeks old, five at the most. Cute little things, of course, and a good pedigree by the look of them.'

'He brought them in for you to have a look at then, did he?'

'Yes. He asked a low price and gave me some cock-and-bull story about them being eight weeks old and fully weaned. I knew they weren't, of course.'

'Any vaccination certificates?'

'No, nothing like that. After I told him no and he took them away again, I had a think and decided to give you a ring.'

'Thanks, Bill. We need more pet-shop owners like you.'

'You mean, someone else might buy the puppies, even if they know they're still too young to leave the mother?' Carly asked.

'If the price is right.' Steve held his pen ready. 'Can you give us any details about the owner?' he asked Bill Brookes.

'He looked like your typical old-age pensioner: shabby green padded jacket, not much hair, a bit overweight. Said his name was Marshall. I asked him where he lived so I could get in touch in three or four weeks when the puppies were ready. He acted a bit odd over that, then scribbled down this address.' Bill pushed a scrap of paper towards Steve. 'He said he didn't have a phone number.'

Steve took the paper and read it. 'Beacon Street. That's not far from here.'

'Hoody lives on that road,' Carly chipped in. 'It runs off the bottom of Beech Hill.'

'I thought it might be worth filling you in,' the pet-shop owner explained. 'There was just something about it that didn't seem right.'

'We'd certainly like to make sure that he doesn't succeed in selling the pups on too soon,' Steve agreed. 'So it looks like we might have to pay him a visit to advise him to hang on to them for a few weeks longer.'

Carly and Steve said goodbye to Bill and all the various talking birds and contented, well-cared-for creatures in their cages. When they got on to the pavement, Carly was anxious. 'What if this Mr Marshall doesn't keep the pups as long as he should?'

Steve took out his car keys and headed for the van. 'At this age, five weeks, they still need to be feeding from the mother. If not, they run the risk of being undersized and miserable, more prone to illness and so on. Any decent pet-shop owner knows that.'

'But if Mr Marshall decides to sell the puppies privately, new owners might not be so well-informed. Again, the pups suffer.' There was one final option that Steve described as they got into the car. 'There again, he might not be able to sell them, and for some reason we don't know about he might not be able to keep them, either.'

'In which case,' Carly broke in, suddenly realising what this meant, 'he would want to get rid of them in whatever way he could!'

This was becoming the day for unwanted animals

and bad owners. As Steve knocked at the door of number 131 Beacon Street, Carly wanted it to be over. She watched him knock again.

Number 131 was a small terraced house with no front garden. The door opened straight on to the pavement. There was no reply, so Steve stepped back and looked up at the bedroom window.

Someone pulled back a blind, then a face appeared. It went away, and soon there was the sound of footsteps coming downstairs. The door opened at last.

'Mr Marshall?' Steve checked the address written on the scrap of paper.

'Who?' The man at the door was young, still half asleep. He scratched his head and blinked at the daylight.

'We're looking for a Mr Marshall. Does he live here?'

The young man shook his head. 'Never heard of him.'

Maybe the number was jotted down wrong, Carly thought.

Steve tried again. 'An oldish chap. He owns

a golden Labrador. You might have seen him taking it for a walk?'

'Not round here, I haven't.' He began to sound short-tempered. 'Listen, I'm on night shift at work. This is supposed to be when I get my sleep!'

'Sorry about that. It's just that Mr Marshall wrote this down as his address.' Steve saw they were up against a dead-end. 'Look, we've obviously been given the wrong information. I'm sorry we woke you up.'

He came back to the van as the man shut the door and went back to bed. 'False trail,' he told Carly.

'What do we do now?'

'There's nothing we *can* do, except hope for the best.'

They drove off up Beacon Street, looking out for an old man walking a Labrador dog, seeing instead women with push-chairs, couples hand in hand, a gang of kids on one corner. 'He lied,' Carly said grimly. 'Why would he do that?'

'He must have something to hide.'

The city traffic snarled them up. They were back on the dual carriageway where they'd found Daisy and her kittens.

'Cheer up,' Steve said. He was going to drop Carly off at Beech Hill before he drove to the local greyhound track to check conditions in the kennels there. 'It might never happen,' he reassured her.

Carly sighed, and got ready to jump out as the van drew up in the carpark. 'That's just it. I think it already has,' she told him.

Her mind was working overtime. Mr Marshall, if that really was his name, didn't want anyone to find him. He had four puppies too young to thrive if he took them away from their mother. He would have his reasons: maybe he was moving house, maybe he was too poor to look after them, or maybe he just didn't care.

Some people didn't. Like Daisy's cruel owner this morning.

But whatever the reason, Carly was worried for those puppies as she walked up the ramp into reception. She had a horrible feeling that before the day was over she would be going out with

ABANDONED

Steve to collect four more abandoned animals, terrified and crying out for help.

5

'Hoody was in here looking for you,' Liz told Carly when she went upstairs to see how Ruby, Jet and Diamond were doing.

'How long ago?' She glanced at her watch. It was half past two: the part of the day when there was a lull between morning and evening surgeries. She knew that her dad and Mel would both be in the operating theatre, carrying out routine operations like dental work and X-rays.

'About ten minutes. When he found out you weren't here, he took Vinny for a walk instead.'

Liz was halfway through feeding the kittens, so Carly lent a hand. 'How do they seem?' She peered into their cage to see Jet's huge yellow eyes staring back at her.

'Still weak. It's partly the shock.' Liz slid her little finger inside Ruby's mouth to show Carly the kitten's gums. 'They're paler than they should be, and her actions are lethargic. It'll take a few days for them to get over it.'

'Will they miss their mother?' Carly picked Jet up and cuddled him.

'Of course. But at five weeks, which is what these kittens are, they're able to lap milk and take some solid food. It would have been worse if they'd been younger.' Liz looked up at Carly. 'Why not let that black one lick from your finger?'

She dipped her forefinger into a dish of milk and offered it to Jet. His rough pink tongue rasped against her skin, greedily lapping up the liquid. She smiled and did it again. 'Ouch! He's got sharp little teeth!'

Liz laughed. 'Give him the whole dish – see if he can manage it.'

So Carly put the shallow dish on to the floor

and set Jet down alongside it. At first he sniffed
and edged away, slipping and sliding on the
shiny white tiles.

She set him right and made him try again.
'Come on, you can do it,' she said softly.

'He's the strongest of the three,' Liz confirmed.
'Just give him a little while to get used to the
idea.'

Jet sniffed again at the milk. He leaned forward
and dipped his nose into it. He wet his whiskers,
lifted his head and shook them. His little black
face looked surprised. Then a drop of milk drib-
bled into his mouth. Out came his tongue, down
went his head. Soon he was lapping contentedly
from the dish.

'That's great,' Liz said. 'With a bit of luck,
they'll survive their terrible experience and live
to fight another day!'

'Your turn!' Carly told Diamond, picking her
up. The kitten trembled and miaowed. But when
she tasted the milk on Carly's finger, then joined
Jet by the dish on the floor, she quietened down.
Within seconds, her pointed tail was wiggling
with pleasure as she drank.

'If I'm worried about any of them, it's this one,' Liz said, showing Ruby's runny eyes and snuffly nose to Carly. 'I don't think it's cat flu; I think it's more likely to be a touch of bronchitis. I sounded her chest and it's congested. Anyway, we'll keep an extra-careful eye on her.' She put the tortoise-shell kitten into the snug blanket on the bottom of the cage. Going to lean her elbows on the windowsill to wait for Diamond and Jet to finish their milk, Liz looked down into the carpark. 'Here come Hoody and Vinny,' she reported. 'But that's funny . . . !'

'What is?' Carly went to join her.

'It's OK, there's nothing wrong with Vinny. Actually, it's what Hoody's doing with his face.'

She looked more closely. 'He's only smiling.'

'Exactly. I've never seen Hoody do that before!' Liz winked and gave Carly a shove. 'Better go and see why!'

So Carly ran downstairs to meet them, waylaying Hoody in reception. 'Why are you smiling?' she demanded.

He stooped to let Vinny off the lead. 'I'm not!'

'No, but you were when you came in. Liz and I wondered what was wrong!'

'Oh, ha-ha!' He was about to turn and go.

'What was that good news you had earlier?' She hadn't seen him since the walk in the park, when she hadn't managed to get it out of him. 'I'll tell you mine if you tell me yours,' she offered.

'You first,' he muttered.

'You're so suspicious! OK, mine is that Jet and Diamond are going to be fine. They're already feeding by themselves. Ruby is a bit weaker. She might have bronchitis. But she'll probably be OK too, in the end!'

Hoody nodded. 'Do you want my good news first, or the bad news?'

She hesitated, then decided. 'The good.'

'Right. It's about Vinny. I've found someone who might take him.'

Carly gasped. 'You mean, give him a home?'

Vinny knew he was being talked about. He wagged his tail and looked up at them.

'It's not definite yet. There's someone on my street who likes dogs. I told him about Vinny being put down tomorrow unless we can find someone to take him. He jumped right in and said he'd have him.'

She could have hugged them both. Instead, she dropped to her knees and spoke to Vinny. 'Did you hear that? Someone wants to adopt you. You're going to have a nice new place to stay!'

'I said "might" take him,' Hoody reminded her. 'I told him he'd have to come in here and fix it up.'

There were adoption papers to sign, a visit to the man's home to see if it was suitable, she realised. 'Did he say he'd come?' she asked, squashing her excitement until they were more sure.

'After tea.'

'That's great. What's this man's name?'

'I haven't a clue. I only know him by sight.' Hoody shrugged his shoulders. 'Anyway, do you want the bad news now?'

Carly stood up. 'About the supermarket box?'

He nodded. 'I haven't found out much. There was a stack of those boxes out at the back. They put them there last night, ready to be crushed and carted off today. That much I do know.'

'Which means the owner of the cats probably picked one up from there either late last night or early this morning?'

'Yeah, but no one I know who works there saw anything. There's a kid from our road who collects trolleys from the carpark and lines them up by the door. He doesn't remember seeing anyone hanging about.'

She nodded. 'Thanks anyway, Hoody.'

'Is that it?' he asked, surprised. 'Are you going to give up?'

'What else can we do?' She'd begun to think that she would have to accept that some owners could just get away with this sort of cruelty. *That's life*. She shrugged.

'We can keep looking.'

'It's like a needle in a haystack . . .' And now there were the four puppies to worry about, and every hour a new problem for the Rescue Centre to sort out.

He stared angrily, ready to go off in another huff.

But she stood in his way and stopped him.

'Listen, Hoody, I don't want us to have an argument. It's been a bad enough day already. But there's a thousand people who could have done it, and what clues have we got? One soggy cardboard box – that's it.'

'No. You know where you found them, on the dual carriageway. You haven't told me where exactly.' He refused to be shaken off.

'Near those new roadworks, just before the traffic lights. Why? What good is that?'

He thought it through. 'If there are roadworks, that means there are men working on the road,' he pointed out. 'They might have seen something!'

She saw what he was getting at. 'You mean, we might get a description of whoever dumped the box?' It was worth a try.

'Or even a name, if we're lucky.'

They ignored the telephone and Paul Grey coming through to reception to answer it.

'What do you think? Are you coming?' Hoody was impatient to be off.

'Wait, I'll tell Dad.'

But when he came off the phone, his face was

serious. 'Hi, Hoody,' he said in a rush. 'Carly, I need some help. I've just had a call about a cat stuck in a tree in the park. Apparently it's injured itself. Steve's still at the greyhound track, so I'll have to go myself. Can you come?'

She glanced at Hoody.

'You go,' he said. 'I can get on better by myself in any case.' He went out before she could argue.

So Carly and her dad ran round the side of the Rescue Centre, down an alleyway into the park. It was easy to see where the injured cat was; a small knot of people had gathered by a gnarled cherry tree that had grown slanted over the years because of the wind. Amongst them there was the anxious owner who had made the phone call, and a crying child.

'Thank goodness!' the woman cried when she saw Paul Grey. 'We don't know what to do. Tabs is caught by his collar. He must have fallen some-how, and the collar got hooked on to the branch!'

They looked up and saw the problem. The cat was stuck high in the tree, well out of reach. 'How long has he been there?' Carly's dad asked.

'We're not sure. He went missing yesterday,

but we've only just found out where he'd got to.'

'He doesn't look very safe,' Carly said quietly. Tabs was half-hanging by his collar, with one leg trapped. He struggled feebly to get back on to the branch.

The girl who was crying overheard and set up a new wail. 'Get him down, please, Mum!' She clung to her mother's hand and stared up through tear-filled eyes.

'What should we do?' The woman turned to Paul Grey. 'I'm afraid that if we try to climb up to rescue him, he'll panic, struggle even harder and topple off the branch!'

'I don't think so.' He decided that the cat was too securely caught by the collar. 'No, we have to go up there for him.'

'I'll go!' Carly was already working out which branches to use. It needed someone light and agile.

So she clambered up the tree, climbing from branch to branch, hearing dead twigs snap and fall, shaking the whole tree as she inched nearer and nearer to Tabs.

The cat saw her and miaowed loudly. But her

dad had been right: he couldn't move. And now that she was closer, Carly saw that the trapped foreleg was rubbed raw. The white fur was red with blood.

'Careful!' Paul Grey warned. 'Will he let you get near him?'

Straddling the branch below the trapped cat, Carly paused. Tabs hissed and struggled to escape one last time. 'It's OK,' she whispered. 'I've come to help!' Gingerly she reached up and took him by the scruff of the neck. Taking his weight, she managed to unhook the collar from the branch.

'OK?' her dad called anxiously.

'Yes, I've got him!' She drew Tabs towards her chest, alarmed at the state of his injured leg as she released it from its unnatural position trapped inside the slim leather collar. The wound was bad: Tabs must have fought to free himself until the collar cut deep into the flesh. Now he howled out loud and trembled.

Down below, his young owner cried with relief.

'How will she climb down?' the mother asked.

Carly was wondering this herself. She needed both hands to tackle the descent.

'See if you can zip him safely inside your jacket!' Paul Grey shouted. 'Then get a move on before he starts to wriggle free!'

She tried it. Carefully she laid the injured cat against her, his head facing towards her chin. Then she fastened the zip so that her jacket formed a kind of cradle for him to rest inside. 'I'm coming down!' she warned.

Swiftly she stood up on the branch and searched for footholds. She felt Tabs squirm. He gave a painful miaow then stayed still. So she made her way down, scratching her hands on the rough bark, half-slipping once as a foothold gave way. But soon she was on firm ground once more.

'Well done!' Paul Grey took the cat and examined the wound. A large patch of fur under the top joint of the leg had been rubbed bare and there was a lot of dried blood. 'We'd better get him back to the surgery,' he advised the woman. 'The wound will need stitches and we'll have to X-ray the leg.'

'Is it broken?' She clutched her little girl's hand and rushed up the hill alongside Carly and Paul Grey. Now that the excitement was over, the interested crowd had begun to disperse.

'It's dislocated at the very least.'

The little girl wailed again; a miserable, worried sound.

'Don't worry,' Carly told her. 'He's just used up one of his lives. Cats have nine, you know!' Bad as it looked, she knew that her dad would be able to treat Tabs and patch him up as good as new.

They took him straight into the prep room, through a still-empty reception and waiting room. Carly helped with the anaesthetic and X-ray, then her father went back out to tell Tabs's owners that the shoulder joint was dislocated but not broken. The whole emergency, including the rescue and the treatment, had taken under an hour, and by the time they had finished and sent Tabs upstairs with Mel to rest and recover in the cat kennels, Hoody had shown up again.

He was hanging about outside the main door,

casually leaning against the handrail at the side of the ramp.

'What are you doing out here?' Carly asked. 'Why didn't you come in?'

He tutted and tilted his head back. 'I could see you were busy. I didn't want to get in the way.'

'Yeah, yeah.' *Let him sulk*, she decided. If he had anything important to tell her about the kittens' owner, let him follow her back inside. She had things to do.

'You were right!' he called after her.

She hesitated and turned. 'How come?'

'No one saw who dumped the box. I asked everyone who was working on the road, and they all said no.' He sounded down in the dumps.

Carly sighed. 'The kittens must have been abandoned during the night, then. That figures. There'd be no one around, so they'd know they wouldn't get caught.' She stopped in the doorway, wondering what Hoody would want to do next.

'That was the bad news . . .' He led her on, using the usual jokey phrase, then shrugging and turning as if he was about to drift off.

Carly could have hit him. 'So what's the good news?' She fell for it, knowing that he loved to make her wait.

'Come and see.' Hoody strolled off across the carpark.

'Not if you don't tell me what it is!' She stayed put, yelling at him over the parked cars.

'Please yourself.' He walked with his hands shoved in his pockets, then he turned to face her. 'I just thought you'd want to come and see the old guy who wants to adopt Vinny, that's all!'

6

'I thought you said he'd come to Beech Hill after tea!' Carly challenged, as Hoody strode on ahead.

'He did. But I've just seen him walking his other dog back home. He said he was really keen to have Vinny. He told me where he lived, so I thought you might want to come and have a look.' Dead casual, take-it-or-leave-it.

So, Vinny's rescuer had another dog for him to make friends with. This wasn't just good news, this was great! 'What's the address?'

'Number 31. He lives at the bottom of my

street. He says he's mad about dogs, has always had one ever since he was a kid.'

'It'll be such a relief if this turns out OK,' Carly said. They turned the corner from Beech Hill on to Beacon Street. 'Vinny will be living close enough for us to see how he's getting on. We could even help to take him for walks!'

Eagerly they read the numbers on the doors, examining the different types of curtains and colours of paint on each of the small terraced houses. Which one would be Vinny's new home?

'This is it, number 31!' Hoody stopped outside a dingy brown door. He knocked loudly then waited.

'At least he lives near the park,' Carly murmured, thinking to herself that the house looked small and cramped. There was no garden to the front, and probably only a yard to the back. 'And I take it he's not out at work all day?' She didn't like the ideas of dogs being cooped up without anyone to keep them company.

'No, he's one of these old, retired sorts.' Hoody knocked again. Inside the house a dog barked and flung itself down the hallway, bouncing up against the locked door and rattling its paws.

'How old?' Carly took a step back. A tiny alarm bell began to sound inside her head.

'I dunno. It's OK, someone's in. I can hear him coming now.'

'What's he look like?'

'Old!' he insisted.

'Is he going bald?' Number 31 Beacon Street. Number 131 Beacon Street. The two addresses could easily be confused. 'Does he wear a green padded jacket?'

'I keep telling you, I've never noticed.' Hoody tried to peer through the letterbox. 'I wish he'd get a move on, though!'

'Down, Bella!' A muffled voice called from the end of the corridor. Steps shuffled towards the door. 'That's a good girl. Yes, yes, I know all about it. Now stop making a fuss!' At last the lock turned and the door opened.

A shabby old man peered out. His head was bald except for tufts of hair over his ears. He wore heavy brown-rimmed glasses with thick lenses, his face was stubbly and lined. 'Oh, it's you,' he muttered when he saw Hoody.

His dog snuffled and scratched at the mat, out of sight. But Carly didn't need to see Bella to know what breed of dog she was.

'Yeah. This is the girl from the Rescue Centre I told you about. Can we come in?'

'Not right now, I'm not ready. You never said.' The old man was flustered by the surprise visit. He made as if to close the door in their faces.

'I didn't think you'd mind. They have to come and check things out, remember.' Hoody began to frown.

'Tomorrow. Come tomorrow. I'm busy.' He struggled to pull Bella out of the way, but the dog was determined to see their visitors. She pushed past him and came out on to the door-step, wagging her tail excitedly.

Carly put a hand to her mouth to hide a groan. Golden Labrador! She knew it. And now she could hear more little paws scuttling down the corridor, small yelps and barks, lots of pushing and shoving.

'What's going on?' Hoody demanded. It sounded like puppies. So why did the old man want to adopt Vinny? Didn't he already have his hands more than full? He leaned on the door to stop him from shutting them out.

'I said, come back later!'

One puppy squeezed through his legs and out into the street. It was a fluffy, pale-yellow miniature of its mother, with big brown eyes and soft paws. Then another escaped, and another. Soon there were four pups playing on the pavement.

Now there was no doubt in Carly's mind. Her hopes for Vinny came crashing down as she stood and confronted the doddery old man. 'Mr Marshall!'

Peering over the top of his glasses, he nodded. 'That's right. How did you know my name?'

'We came looking for you earlier today,' Paul Grey explained. Carly and Hoody had gone straight home to speak to her dad, and he'd come back with them to number 31 Beacon Street. This time they'd all been invited inside the house and were sitting in the cold back kitchen, trying to sort things out. 'One of our inspectors got your name from Bill Brookes at Pampered Pets. We needed to tell you that it's too soon to try and sell the pups. They should stay with their mother for another few weeks yet.'

Bella had sidled up to Carly to be stroked. She was overweight, like old Mr Marshall, but good-natured and friendly. Hoody took one of the puppies on to his knee, while the other three played under the table. Meanwhile Paul Grey talked on.

He produced a scrap of paper from his pocket and laid it flat. 'Unfortunately, the address looks like 131 instead of 31, so we couldn't find you.'

Mr Marshall peered short-sightedly and jabbed with his finger. 'That's not a 1. It's a line. "Marshall/31 Beacon Street", see?' He pushed the paper back towards Paul.

'Right. Anyway, the fact remains: Bella should keep the youngsters until they're properly weaned.'

'What's that? I'm a bit hard of hearing?' The old man cupped his ear with his hand. 'You're saying I should let Bella go, too?'

'No!' Carly's dad hid his impatience. 'Not at all. I'm sure Bella is perfectly happy here with you.'

'She's a fine dog,' the old man agreed. 'We're best mates, me and Bella. But I find the pups too much of a handful if you want to know the truth. They get under my feet. I'm afraid that one of these days I'm going to trip up and take a fall. I don't see too well, you know.'

'I understand that.' Paul Grey spoke up loud and clear. 'I also hear you were thinking of adopting another dog?'

'I would like one,' he confessed. 'But I couldn't have the puppies around much longer if I took another, could I?' Mr Marshall gave a confused sigh. 'Oh dear, now I don't know what to think!'

Carly patted Bella and stooped to pick up another of the pups. They had blunt, round faces and droopy ears. Their stumpy tails wagged to and fro.

'Do you get any help around the house?' Mr Grey asked, looking round at the unwashed pots and piles of old newspapers stacked on chairs.

Carly noticed that the old gas cooker was thick with grease. An ancient wall clock had stopped at five to ten.

'Help? You mean help with the cleaning? No!

But I manage,' the old man insisted. 'Me and Bella get on perfectly well, thank you.'

Carly's dad thought hard, then stood up. 'I'll tell you what, Mr Marshall. I can think of one way we could ease the problem about the pups. We run a Rescue Centre at Beech Hill as well as a surgery. We could take the puppies out of your way, up to the Centre. You can call by with Bella a couple of times each day so she can go on feeding them. That way, everyone will be happy!'

'Come again?' He cupped his ear and frowned.

'We'll look after the pups for you!' Paul Grey almost shouted.

'Yes, but would I still get my money for them?'

'I don't see why not. When the pups reach eight or nine weeks, we'll see that they're properly vaccinated, then send them off to Pampered Pets. I'm sure Bill won't have any problem selling them once they're old enough.'

The old man nodded. 'I could do with a bit of extra cash.'

'Quite right. Is that OK, then?'

He nodded. 'It'll be a relief, to tell you the truth. I'd be grateful if you could take them and keep them safe. Even Bella's getting a bit fed up with having them clamouring round her all the time. This is her third litter, and she's not so young as she used to be.'

'Well, no time like the present.' Paul took one pup from Carly and told her and Hoody to gather up the other three. 'We'll take them and settle them in at our place. You and Bella could call round after tea,' he suggested. He paused, then went on. 'As for this other dog . . .'

'The stray?' Mr Marshall squinted at Hoody, remembering his earlier promise.

'Yes – Vinny. I've a feeling he'd be too much of a handful for you under the circumstances.' Paul Grey tried to let him down gently. 'One dog's enough, don't you think?'

'It would have been nice, though.' The old man shook his head sadly. 'A friend for Bella!'

'But two dogs to take for walks. Another mouth to feed. And the one we're talking about is a tough customer. He's full of energy, needs lots of exercise. I really don't think you could manage.'

'Perhaps you're right,' came the slow reply.

Carly had gathered the pups and stood next to Hoody, waiting for the old man to see the light. No way could he take on Vinny. Hoody's solution was crumbling to bits in front of their eyes.

'Never mind, Mr Marshall, you just concentrate on taking good care of Bella,' Paul Grey advised. 'Forget everything else. Labradors make wonderful, gentle pets, and they're easy to look after. In fact, they're one of my favourite breeds. Just go on enjoying her company.'

They made their way out of the kitchen, along the narrow corridor towards the front door. Bella plodded along beside them, looking up at her pups, but not distressed to see them go. She'd obviously done her bit. Now it was someone else's turn to lend a hand.

So that was that. They were out on the pavement carrying the pups in their arms, saying goodbye to old Mr Marshall and Bella, fostering four new charges instead of getting rid of one. There was no home here for Vinny after all.

'How was I to know!' Hoody protested, walking head down, shoulders hunched, along Beech Hill with Carly and Paul Grey. 'I didn't have a clue he was some nutty old man who can't even look after the animals he's already got!'

'It's not your fault,' Carly agreed. 'He should never have offered in the first place.' She carried two of the pups, snuggling one under each arm.

'There's no point blaming Mr Marshall either,' Paul Grey reminded her. 'It's never as straight-forward as it looks. It's not a question of him not caring. I'm sure he'd have done his best to give Vinny a good home, but it would have been beyond him. It wouldn't have been fair.'

'Poor Vinny,' Carly sighed. It was teatime. The hours were slipping by, and now there was less than a day to find him a good home before the final deadline.

Hoody fell silent, brooding over the problem. 'I should have realised, though. I mean, think of Vinny, then look at Mr Marshall. Anyone can see it wouldn't have worked.'

'Yes, Vinny needs someone young with as much energy as he's got,' Paul Grey said as they reached the Rescue Centre. 'An outdoors sort of owner who's ready to take him for long walks,

throw sticks for him, keep him under control.'
He stared long and hard at Hoody himself.

'Don't look at me!' Hoody coloured up and
shoved the pup he was carrying into Mr Grey's
arms. He knitted his brows and looked down at
his boots, then turned abruptly on his heel and
walked off, leaving them stranded outside the
main entrance.

'What did I say?' Paul Grey asked, raising his
eyebrows.

Carly backed through the door with her two
pups. 'Nothing. Ignore him.'

'I must have said something to upset him,' Paul
insisted, following her inside.

'There's no point hoping that Hoody would be
able to have Vinny,' she explained. 'I'm sure he'd
love to. But he lives with his sister, Zoe. And
Zoe's boyfriend, Dean, hates dogs, so there's no
chance.' Suggesting it had only made it worse.

'Trust me to put my foot in it.' They went to
show the new pups to Liz and Mel, but Carly's
dad still had his mind on his own tactlessness.
'Poor Hoody,' he said. 'I never knew that. What
happened to his parents?'

'He doesn't get on with them. He gets on OK with Zoe, though.' Hoody didn't often talk about himself, but she knew this much.

'That must be tough.' Paul Grey studied Carly's face. 'Are you OK?'

'Disappointed,' she admitted.

'Tired?'

'Yep.'

'Worried about Vinny?'

' . . . and Ruby and Jet and Diamond. And the four pups. And Tabs. And Brandy . . .'

It had been one of those days. Only a late supper nestled on the sofa in front of the TV could ease Carly's worries. Then a long, long rest. She went to bed and fell asleep dreaming of kittens playing on a daisy-covered lawn in front of a thatched cottage in the country with smiling owners looking on . . .

7

By next morning Bella's pups had made themselves completely at home. Carly had chosen a special place for them, in a box in the laundry room, where it was warm and cosy. Old Mr Marshall had been as good as his word and brought Bella in to feed them the night before. Now they were scampering everywhere, clamouring for a more solid breakfast of easy-to-digest puppy food.

'Hold your horses!' Carly pleaded. They wove in and out of her legs as she carried food dishes to the rows of kennels that backed on to the exercise yard. 'These aren't for you!'

Smiling at their antics, she took care to keep them in isolation. Until they'd had their health jabs, she had to make sure they stayed away from the other dogs. She opened up a kennel and put a dish down for Vinny. He knew the routine and stood patiently to one side. 'That's a good boy,' she said softly. The metal dish clinked against the concrete floor and the dog dived for the food.

Try not to think ahead, Carly told herself, firmly closing the kennel door. *Vinny doesn't know what lies in store for him later today. He's perfectly happy eating his breakfast.* She went on to Brandy's kennel and placed another dish down for him.

The guide dog sat quietly in the far corner, watching without moving.

'Here you are, boy!' She rattled the dish. Still no response. 'What's wrong? Aren't you hungry?' Carly knew the signs. Poor Brandy was pining for Harmony. 'Never mind, it won't be long now,' she promised. His mistress was due out of hospital later today. By tonight, Brandy should be safely back home.

Next she fed the Border collie pups, then the cruelty case in kennel five. Soon everyone was feeding happily.

Then it was time to hose down the yard; a job that Carly always did for Mel during the school holidays. She put on her wellies, aiming the strong jet into every corner.

Then the cages in the small pets' room had to be cleaned out and relined with newspaper and straw. Today there was a moulting parrot squawking from his perch, two guinea-pigs and a white rabbit with black markings and silky black ears. She was deep in conversation with the friendly parrot when Liz popped her head around the door and reminded her that it was time to feed Diamond, Jet and Ruby yet again.

'I know, it seems as if they've got hollow legs!' She grinned. 'But if they're always hungry, that means they're doing well. We should be thankful.'

'I am,' Carly admitted as she took the stairs two at a time. Glancing down into reception, she saw that the waiting room was already crowded with patients and their owners. 'I can manage by myself,' Carly told Liz.

'Sure?' The young vet had a busy morning ahead. She thanked Carly and went to begin on her list of patients. But at the bottom of the stairs she paused and called up. 'You've got a visitor, Carly!'

'Who is it?' Whoever it was, she didn't have time to stop and chat. She took a packet of powdered milk from a shelf and began to mix it with water, ready to pour into dishes.

'It's me.' Hoody appeared in the doorway. 'I came to take Vinny for a walk.'

Carly stopped what she was doing and shot him a quick look. 'You know what day it is, don't you?'

He nodded. 'Don't remind me.'

There was a heavy silence as they stood and recognised that hope had almost faded for the unwanted stray. Then Carly pointed to the cage where Jet, Diamond and Ruby were miaowing loudly. 'If you give me a hand here, I'll come with you,' she said quietly.

So tough Hoody opened the cage and gingerly

lifted the first tiny kitten out. It was Jet, opening his mouth wide and yowling with all his might.

'Why's he making such a racket?' Hoody held him at arm's length.

'He's letting us know he's hungry.' Carly tried not to smile. Hoody looked like a fish out of water, grimacing at Jet as the kitten squirmed and yelled. 'Put him down on the floor.' She poured the warm milk into the dish and placed it on the floor. The moment Jet saw and smelt it, the crying stopped.

'Phew.' Hoody relaxed as he watched the kitten lap the milk. 'What about this one?' He took Diamond out of the cage. This time he held the kitten more confidently.

'Here's her dish.' Carly put a second metal saucer on the floor. Soon both kittens were guzzling it all up.

'And this one?' Hoody had picked Ruby up and was stroking her softly.

Carly went over. 'No, Ruby isn't as fit as the other two. We think she's got a chest infection. She's not lapping properly yet. We'd better hand-feed her. You hold on to her while I get the pipette ready.'

Hoody bent his crew-cut head over the brown tortoiseshell kitten. 'I'm still looking, you know,' he muttered.

'What for?' At first Carly thought he meant a home for poor Vinny.

'For the lousy person who dumped them in the first place,' he said angrily. 'I've been asking around and I did hear of a cat with some kittens. They were living in a shed at the bottom of the allotments off King Edward's Road.'

Carly took Ruby and showed Hoody how to persuade the kitten to open her mouth so that they could begin feeding her. 'Do you want to have a go?'

He nodded and sat on a stool, taking Ruby awkwardly on to his knee.

'You mean, this allotment cat was living wild?' Carly said. It was something they hadn't considered so far.

'Sort of. Someone must have been feeding her, though.'

'But she didn't have an owner?' It made sense: Daisy had been a stray, what they called a feral cat living off the leftovers of city life, scrounging food wherever she could. It would explain why no one had brought her to a vet to be spayed, why she'd had kittens when she was so young herself, and why there was no one to look after her and help her take care of the kittens once they were born.

'I guess so. But someone must have got fed up when the kittens came along. They didn't fancy having their allotment overrun with cats. So they put them in a cardboard box and dumped them.'

Carly frowned. Hoody was managing in a clumsy way to get the milk into Ruby's mouth, but the kitten wasn't keen to swallow. 'Maybe you're right.'

'I know I am! King Edward's Road leads straight on to the dual carriageway. Whoever did it could just stick them in a box, sling it in the back of his car and drive up on to the main road. Simple!'

'But how would you prove it?' She offered to take Ruby from him.

'I don't know yet. All I know is, there was a cat with kittens living down there, and now there isn't.' Hoody went to look out of the first-floor window. 'I'll prove it,' he promised, cool and determined.

Meanwhile, they had to try and get Ruby to feed. Carly tilted her chin and began to stroke her throat. This should encourage her to swallow, she knew. Even if she just took a little, it would help keep her strength up. Patiently Carly tried again with the dropper. This time the kitten felt the milk land on her tongue and gulped. 'Good girl,' she said, still stroking her soft throat. 'Now try again.'

'I don't know how you can stand living here,' Hoody said suddenly, still staring out of the window. 'It would drive me mad!'

'Why?' For her it was normal. She never even thought about it. 'Do you mean the noise and stuff?' It was true, there were always dogs barking, cats miaowing, phones ringing, cars arriving and setting off in the middle of the night.

'No, I mean dealing with things getting sick and dying. And people dumping animals on you. And not having enough room to keep them for ever. That kind of stuff.'

She knew he meant Daisy and the kittens, the

Labrador pups, Vinny. 'It's not all bad,' she reminded him. 'Sometimes the animals get better. In fact, most of the time. And usually we do find good homes.'

'Not this time,' he reminded her.

Vinny – this was what was really bothering him. She put the milk dropper back into the dish and pushed her hair behind her ears. 'This time, maybe not.'

'Are you sure there's nothing we can do?' He turned and pushed himself clear of the window-sill, beginning to pace up and down the room.

'Mind Jet and Diamond!' Carly warned. The kittens had finished feeding and were chasing their own tails and scampering here and there. She put Ruby back into the cage and went to pick them up. 'We've tried everything. The trouble is, we have to wait for people to show up here and offer to take our animals away from us. If they don't, we're stuck.'

'You mean, there might be people out there who want a kitten like one of these, or a puppy like one of Bella's, but they don't know you're here?' It struck Hoody for the first time that the

Rescue Centre relied on new owners finding out about the homeless pets and coming to volunteer.

'Well, we're in the phone book,' Carly pointed out. 'We're listed as Beech Hill Animal Home and Clinic.'

'But you wait for them to come to you?' he insisted.

'I suppose so. We don't advertise, if that's what you mean. We couldn't afford to do that.' Most of the money needed to run the Centre came from charity, or from grateful pet owners who left gifts in their wills. 'Anyway, most of the time we do get a steady trickle of people who want to adopt our pets. We're not always as full as this. In fact, usually we even have a waiting list.'

Hoody shook his head. 'I'm not talking about usually. I'm talking about now!'

'I know. But we can't suddenly magic owners out of thin air.' She put Jet, then Diamond, safely back in the cage, and made a note on the white-board to tell Mel what time the kittens had been fed.

'We could make out cards, put notices in the supermarket, the paper shop and everywhere.

You know: "Wanted, Good Homes for Unwanted Dogs and Cats. Urgent!" ' Hoody was saying the first things that came into his head. 'Come on, Carly, where are the felt-tips? Get a move on!'

'OK!' It sounded like a good idea. She opened a drawer and took out a pile of postcards and some pens. She began to work out exactly what they should write down, noticing that Hoody could design artistic lettering. She let him get on with the job of writing it down.

'Everything OK up here?' Paul Grey put his head around the door in passing. He was carrying the half-bald parrot down to a treatment room.

'Yep. Hoody's had this great idea of putting cards up in the shops to advertise for owners!'

'Good thinking. We're bursting at the seams at the moment. We do have to do something extra-special to solve the problem.' He went on his way, trying to quieten the noisy bird.

Carly took each card as Hoody finished it and coloured in some of the letters. 'Ready?' she asked at last.

He nodded. 'This had better work!'

He was rushing ahead, leaping down the stairs, already at the door when Carly followed him into reception.

' . . . Yes, I know you've rung three times already!' Bupinda was saying in an exasperated voice. 'I have tried to speak to Paul and Liz about it. But there's only a limited number of hours in every day, and to be quite honest we don't have the time to invite TV cameras in . . . we're rushed off our feet . . . sorry!'

Carly stopped in her tracks. She'd just had a brain-wave. Before Bupinda could put down the phone, she ran and seized it.

'Hello, this is Carly Grey here. I'm Paul Grey's daughter. I hear you want to come and film the animals in the Rescue Centre? That sounds great. When would you like to come?'

8

'I'm sorry I didn't tell you what I was doing,' Carly told Bupinda after she'd put down the phone. 'There wasn't time!'

'What did they say?' Hoody wanted to know.

Carly was bubbling with excitement, but trying to keep her voice down so the news didn't spread too quickly around the waiting room. 'They said they were from the local news team. They're doing a slot on abandoned animals and they found our number in the phone book. They were beginning to give up hope of ever getting in to film us though.'

'They sound as if they're in a hurry.' Hoody had watched her grab the opportunity to bring the TV cameras in without fully understanding why.

'They are. They want to put the news item out this evening, after the main news!' It had come to her in a flash – why bother with single postcards in shop windows, when you could have Jet's sweet little face staring out of every television screen in the area?

'So when are they coming in?'

Carly looked at her watch. It was still only ten o'clock. 'After lunch. They said at about half past one. They're sending a camera and a sound man, and that woman reporter who reads the news most nights.'

'Andrea Whitemore?' Bupinda forgave Carly and pricked up her ears. 'I like her!'

'They'll want to interview Dad and Liz about the work we do, then they'll take lots of films of the animals.'

'I get it. You think showing them on the telly will make loads of people ring up?' Hoody's frown lightened and changed to a grin. 'Hey, that's brilliant!'

Carly blushed. 'It's great publicity, isn't it? And it's happening at exactly the right time!'

'Aren't you forgetting one thing?' Bupinda grew sensible once more. She was the one who kept them all organised with her quiet, efficient manner and tidy, precise mind. 'You haven't asked your father yet.'

'There wasn't time.' Carly had jumped in with both feet.

'There never is with you,' Bupinda grumbled. 'Once you get something in your head, you go for it no matter what.'

'Don't you think it'll work?' she faltered. The receptionist was pulling her back to earth with a bump.

'I think it will!' Hoody barged in, ready to stick up for her.

'Calm down. I never said it wouldn't.' Bupinda switched on the intercom into Paul's treatment room. 'I only said you need to ask him if it's OK first.'

'Ask me if what's OK?' the familiar voice came back. It was Carly's dad speaking into the phone.

She swallowed hard and grabbed Hoody's

arm. 'Come with me,' she pleaded.

So they went to find Paul Grey, busy hacking small lumps of yellow deposit from between the sharp teeth of a German shepherd dog which had been anaesthetised in room number three.

'This is what happens if you don't take care of a dog's dental hygiene!' he mumbled, digging out the plaque with a sharp hooked instrument. The big dog lay senseless, but he would soon wake up with a sore mouth.

'Dad, can we ask you a favour?' Carly began nervously.

'Sure, fire away.'

'Would you mind if some visitors came in to take a look round later today?' She tried to break it to him gradually. 'They wouldn't be any trouble, honestly. They've promised to stay in the background and just let you get on as normal.'

'Fine.' That sort of thing didn't bother him. He often had students and work-experience kids in to see what went on.

Carly cleared her throat then went on. 'So would it be OK if they brought a camera in with them?'

'Sure. No problem.' He worked on, cleaning the dog's teeth.

'And a microphone, and just one reporter?'

Paul Grey stood up straight. 'Reporter?' he echoed. 'Who *are* these people?'

The time had come to confess everything. 'They're from the local TV station. They want to do a kind of fly-on-the-wall film: you know, show everything as it really is. And Hoody and I thought it would help just now because we've got this overcrowding problem, and people will be able to see who needs a new home and they can ring us up and . . .'

'Steady!' Paul Grey had listened long enough. 'I get the picture.'

'Is it OK?' Hoody spoke for the first time. 'The thing is, it would be Vinny's last chance.'

'In what way?' Carly's dad considered things carefully.

'We'd ask them to film Vinny specially; kind of make him the star of the show, explain that he'll have to be put down if someone doesn't ring up to take him today. Get it?'

Paul Grey nodded. 'It's still a very big "if",' he

warned. 'Vinny's always going to be a difficult animal to find a home for. He'll be up alongside all the cute puppies and kittens.'

'We know that.' Hoody stuck to his guns.

'You two would have to do all the extra grooming and cleaning involved. If we allow a TV camera in, the whole place will have to be spotless.'

They both nodded, rooted to the spot. '*Say yes!*' Carly pleaded silently.

'OK, go ahead,' her dad said at last. 'It's a great idea, but as you can see I'm busy. I'll leave it all up to you!'

'Stand still, Brandy!' Carly began grooming Harmony Brown's wonderfully obedient dog. 'This is how it's done!' she explained to Vinny, who sulked inside his kennel. No one was going to rub him and brush him and make *him* stand still to have his eyes and ears wiped clean!

Brandy's light-brown coat glowed with health. Carly drew the brush over its thick surface. 'Good boy! We're going to make you look beautiful for the camera. Everyone's going to see you at your best!' She worked hard with the brush until her arm began to ache.

'I'll do Vinny,' Hoody suggested. He'd been watching Carly until he got the hang of it. 'Come on, you heard what she said,' he told the reluctant dog. 'You're gonna get groomed whether you like it or not!'

He picked the dog up by wrapping his arms around his legs and carrying him to a table. 'Stay!' he said while he reached for a metal comb.

Vinny jumped off and skulked in the corner.

'Chicken!' Hoody put him back on. This time he held him firmly in place.

Vinny saw the brush and let his head droop. He pulled away to the edge of the table.

'Come on, this is important!' Hoody insisted. He began to brush the short hair along Vinny's back. 'This dog stinks!' he complained.

'Give him a bath,' Carly suggested. She was teasing out a couple of knots in the longer hair on Brandy's belly.

'You must be joking. I'm having enough trouble as it is, without trying to stick him in a bath full of soapy water. How about a wipe down with this damp cloth instead?'

She said that would be OK. It was a pity that Vinny himself didn't think so. He saw the cloth coming towards him and dived off the table, then under it. Carly laughed at Hoody's face.

'This isn't funny. We've got to get him looking decent for the camera.' He glared at the scruffy dog with its brown and black stripes, its flash of white on the chest. 'What kind of mixture do you think he is?' he asked.

'He's all sorts. A bit of boxer, a bit of greyhound maybe.' His chest was deep, his front legs wide apart. But he was narrow at the back, with a long, thin tail. 'I've finished here. Shall I have a go for you?' she offered.

But Hoody was set on grooming Vinny himself. He shook his head and lifted him back on to the table for a third time, getting him into a sort of headlock and whisking the wet cloth over his dull coat.

'Talk to him. Tell him he's being a good boy,' Carly suggested. 'Dogs like that.'

Already red in the face with the effort of holding him and wiping at the same time, Hoody grunted. 'Good boy.'

Vinny squirmed and backed out of his grip.

'Here, boy!' Carly let Brandy jump down from his table. She put the grooming brush into his mouth and asked him to take it to Hoody. The Labrador behaved like an absolute dream.

'Good boy!' Hoody hung on fast to Vinny. 'You're not going to get out of this, so don't think you are!' He took the brush from Brandy and began again on Vinny.

Gradually he was getting somewhere. Vinny stopped struggling and stood still while he was brushed. 'Yeah, yeah, I know; you think this is no good. Only nerds and geeks have their hair brushed, not tough dogs like you. But we've got our reasons, so you just have to grin and bear it, OK?' Hoody spoke all the time he was working, holding on to the dog's collar with one hand and working his way down from head to tail with the other.

In the end Vinny looked halfway decent. Hoody let him go and went on to help Carly groom Bella's pups.

'Even though we don't actually need homes for these just yet, they'll make everybody watching the programme go "Aah!" and that's exactly what we want,' Carly explained. 'Then they'll be paying attention when we show Vinny and the other dogs.'

'What about the sheepdog pups?' Hoody was watching Carly and copying her. He wiped one of the pup's eyes with cotton wool, then rubbed it all over with a damp towel.

'We still need homes for two of them.' She went to the kennel and brought one back. The little black-and-white dog bared his teeth and barked at the mini Bellas. 'Who's a fierce little thing?' She held him up in both hands and rocked him gently. With his deep-brown eyes, black ears and fluffy white muzzle, she knew they would have no trouble getting viewers to adore him. Meanwhile, two of the other collies squeezed out after him and came and tugged at the bottom of Hoody's jeans.

'Watch out!' The puppies had made him jump. But he looked down at his feet and grinned.

'They're trying to herd you!' The two little

pups growled and worried at Hoody's trainers. 'Aren't they sweet? I wish the cameras were already here!'

'Don't they know I'm not a sheep?' He laughed as they shuffled backwards and crouched low, as if waiting for him to do as he was told.

'What time is it?' Carly looked at her watch, shocked to see that it was nearly one o'clock. Only thirty minutes to go. She began to shoo the puppies and dogs back into their kennels, ready for the TV crew to arrive. 'I have to feed the kittens before they get here!' she remembered. 'And clean them up to make them look their best.' The film was a good chance to get owners to sign up for Jet, Diamond and Ruby, too.

So she ran to do that while Hoody swept the corridors and cleaned the yard. She saw her dad busy in the office, clutching a cup of coffee in one hand while he used the phone. Bupinda tidied her already-tidy desk in reception. Liz was checking drugs in the drugs cabinets, ready for evening surgery, while Mel disappeared into the ladies toilet to do her hair.

'It's not only the animals who have to look

102

good!' she told Carly. There was her long red hair to tie up, her lipstick to renew.

Grinning, Carly ran to see to the kittens. This was like getting ready for a visit from royalty: everything clean and sparkling, everyone on their best behaviour. Except her and Hoody. She just had time to feed the three cats and put them back in their cosy cage, then shoot down to help Hoody finish off in the yard. He was whooshing jets of water across the concrete, washing away the disinfectant when she came up from behind.

'Hurry up, they'll be here any minute!' she warned.

He jumped and turned, the hose still in his hand. *Whoosh!* It squirted right at her.

'Aagh!' She leaped to one side, not quite quickly enough. The water drenched her jeans.

'Sorry!' In his surprise, Hoody dropped the hose. It carried on squirting a fast jet of water, snaking wildly around the yard, soaking his own feet and legs.

Carly dived for the tap and turned it off. The hose stopped shooting water everywhere. But it was too late. Carly felt her jeans drip. She wiped her hands on her sweater and pushed stray locks of hair back from her wet face. She looked aghast at Hoody. He too was dripping from head to foot.

'They're here!' Mel called from her lookout position on the first floor. She looked like a cover girl with her smart hair and new make-up. 'Their van's just turned into the carpark!'

Bupinda arranged leaflets in the rack by the door. Liz put on a clean white coat and Paul Grey straightened his tie. 'Come on, you two!' he called to Carly and Hoody. 'What on earth are you doing out there? The filming's about to begin. Get a move on or you'll miss all the excitement!'

9

'It's time!' Mel had been waiting for the signature tune since before five o'clock. The TV crew had been and gone, they'd interviewed everyone at Beech Hill, including Carly, and promised that they would be making a five-minute item about them for the news that evening. Now the local programme was about to begin.

'Come on, everybody!' Paul Grey had invited the whole rescue team up to the flat. The television was on, the theme tune was playing.

Steve Winter had come back to the Centre

during the middle of filming with yet another neglected dog. The cameraman had filmed everything as it happened; he'd captured the animal's misery as Steve led it in, its matted hair, its sticking-out ribs. Beech Hill's inspector had made the cruel owner sign the papers to hand the dog over into their care. Now Steve was watching to see how it came across on TV.

Mel had played her part during the filming, too. She was everywhere at once, bustling through the treatment rooms with patients, handing instruments to Liz in the operating theatre. 'I'm sure I looked a complete mess!' she said now, as she settled down on the Greys' sofa to watch the programme.

Liz kidded her along. She herself had been almost too busy to notice the camera. She'd given an interview about her own upbringing in the Scottish Borders, where she'd lived on a farm and learned an early love of all animals. 'Come and sit here,' she told Bupinda, when she noticed her hovering in the background. 'There's plenty of room.'

The receptionist joined the eager audience.

'Come on, Paul. It's started!' She wanted
all to see it from the beginning. Here was And
Whitemore reading the news and introducing the
items in tonight's programme.

'Coming!' He carried a tray of coffee mugs
from the kitchen into the living room, just at the
moment when Andrea announced the piece
about them.

'And tonight,' she said in her relaxed and
friendly style, 'we have a special item high-
lighting some of the work that goes on locally to
rescue and protect the neglected pets of our
region. Stay with us for a visit to Beech Hill
Rescue Centre, later in the programme.'

'Quick, where's Carly?' Mel asked, suddenly
realising that she was missing. Everyone looked
round to see where she'd got to.

'Over here.' She'd stayed by the door with
Hoody. He was refusing to come all the way into
the room, saying he could hardly bear to watch.

'What if this doesn't work?' he whispered.

They'd put their hearts and souls into it, first
getting the animals ready, then showing the TV
people round the Centre. Now for the first time

they both stopped to think what it all meant.

'It will work,' Carly promised. It *had* to. People would be sitting down to their meals watching this programme. They would see all the good work that went into rescuing the strays and the animals that owners could no longer care for. They would realise that many lovely pets were in desperate need of new homes. The programme would end. Then the phone at Beech Hill would begin to ring with a flood of offers.

'Quiet now, people!' Mel hushed them. 'I think this is us!'

'It goes without saying that we British are a nation of animal lovers,' Andrea began, looking earnestly into the camera from behind her pale-blue desk. She was dressed in a navy-blue suit with a neat white blouse. Her dark hair was newly combed and styled. 'Or does it? I must admit, it was something I took for granted until earlier today, when I dropped in on veterinary surgeon, Paul Grey, at his unique animal rescue centre.'

'That's us!' Bupinda pointed to the picture on the screen of the outside of Beech Hill. The big

Victorian house with its modernised main entrance looked strange on TV. 'There I am!' she cried, as the camera drew the viewer inside and showed them the reception area.

Cut to Andrea, dressed more casually in a wax jacket and colourful silk scarf, showing the viewer round the Centre. 'Here, behind its calm Victorian façade, lies a daily round of coping with cruelty and neglect.'

From the back of the room Carly narrowed her eyes to catch sight of a shot of Tabs with his raw wound, newly stitched, then of Jet, Ruby and Diamond in their cage. The camera stopped on them and went in close.

'These kittens, only a few weeks old, were brought in yesterday by Paul's daughter, Carly, and inspector Steve Winter. They'd been found abandoned in a cardboard box, alongside their mother, whom the Beech Hill staff christened Daisy.' Andrea's voice grew more serious still. 'Daisy's case is all too typical. Neglected and ill, unable to look after her kittens, she was so weak when she arrived here at Beech Hill that an emergency operation failed to save her life. Now the orphaned kittens, Ruby, Diamond and Jet, must be hand-reared.'

The camera switched to Carly feeding Ruby from the glass dropper. The tortoiseshell kitten opened her mouth to let the milk trickle in, then she licked Carly's hand with her little pink tongue.

Andrea's voice spoke on over the scene. 'In a few weeks, with the skill of the Beech Hill team behind them, the three kittens hopefully will have recovered from their ordeal and be ready to go out to new homes.'

Switch now to a shot of the dog kennels, with Brandy sitting patiently gazing out through the bars, and the litter of Border collie pups romping and playing. Then to the laundry room, with Bella's puppies tugging at a pile of towels and running in-between table legs.

'As will these adorable little Labrador pups . . .' Andrea went on to explain their background. Two of the puppies came inquisitively up to the camera, heads to one side, to investigate what it was.

'Paul Grey, Director of the Centre, promises us

that most prospective owners who ring up Beech Hill will find the kittens and puppies irresistible. Isn't that true, Paul?'

The camera cut away from Andrea and on to Carly's dad. Carly smiled to see his face on the screen. He looked serious and kind at the same time, not at all embarrassed by the camera.

'We generally have no trouble finding homes for young animals like these,' he agreed. 'However, we always give a complete set of injections against disease and make a thorough check to see that everything is OK and conditions are suitable before we let them go.' He walked on with Andrea, out into the reception area, where the camera caught a glimpse of Hoody and Carly standing with Vinny.

Carly squirmed to see herself on TV. She still looked damp from her soaking in the yard, and beside Hoody she seemed small and young. They were both pretending to ignore the camera, but not succeeding very well at all.

'There you are!' Mel called to Hoody over the commentary.

'Ssh!' Bupinda said.

'Unfortunately it's not the same story for older dogs and cats,' Paul Grey was telling Andrea. 'Dogs like Vinny, for instance. They're much more difficult to place.'

'Why's that?'

'People generally want young dogs which they can train themselves. It's understandable, but it gives us a problem which we can't always solve, like with Vinny here.'

There was a close-up of Vinny staring straight into the camera lens, looking ready to jump down the cameraman's throat.

'Yes?' Andrea prompted. 'Tell us, what exactly *is* Vinny's story?'

Carly could remember her dad's answer word for word. She heard it again now as the item went out on air to hundreds of thousands of homes.

'Vinny's been at Beech Hill for over six weeks now. Since he's been here we've been lucky enough to return him to full health and fitness. But this is a photograph of Vinny when he first arrived.'

He held up a picture and the camera zoomed in. The photograph showed a dog who was skeleton-thin, with sores and scabs all over his body. He was filthy dirty, with eyes red and weeping from infection.

Carly heard Hoody draw an angry breath. He was shocked by the photo of Vinny in his original state, but Carly remembered it all too well.

'And what do you think had happened to him?' Andrea Whitemore asked.

'We don't know exactly. Steve picked him up on one of the high-rise estates. No collar, no clues as to where he'd come from. Presumably he did have an owner once. But whoever it was must have got tired of looking after him. Or else they moved on and couldn't take him with them. Or they fell ill themselves. There are many reasons why people abandon dogs like Vinny.'

'And what now?'

The camera was back on a fit and healthy Vinny in reception, getting up impatiently and waiting at the door to be taken for a walk.

'We've had him six weeks, as I said. That's about as long as we can have a dog cooped up in the conditions in our kennels here. Our animal behaviourist tells us that it's mentally cruel to keep them any longer.' Paul Grey paused and sighed. 'So, with Vinny, we've reached the point where we've had to make a hard decision.'

'Meaning what exactly?' The camera went back to Andrea, then on to Paul.

'Meaning that, unless we manage to find him a home as a result of this programme, I'm afraid he will have to be humanely destroyed.'

Bupinda and Mel manned the phones in reception, while Liz, Paul, Carly and Hoody hovered anxiously nearby.

'We'll write down all the names and phone numbers.' Bupinda got organised with paper and pen, waiting for the avalanche of calls.

Everyone agreed that the news item had come over well. Andrea Whitemore had ended it by letting people know how to go about adopting any of the animals they'd seen. The information had come up on screen – Beech Hill's address and phone number.

'Tell everyone that we'll put their name on a list, with details of the type of animal they're looking for,' Paul told Bupinda. 'We won't be able to give then an answer right away, but say we'll get back to them as soon as we can.'

'And say they might not get the one they saw on TV, but there are always plenty more cats and dogs waiting for good homes. Ask them if they're willing to leave their name on a waiting list,' Liz reminded them.

Carly paced up and down beside the desk. 'Ring!' she pleaded to the still-silent phone.

'Give them time to finish their tea,' her dad said. He seemed calm and confident. He turned back to Mel and Bupinda. 'Oh, and tell them they can come to the Centre tomorrow morning to take a proper look at the animals that are up for adoption. That'll give us a chance to assess them too.'

The plan was made. Everyone understood.

'Ring!' Carly hissed at the phone. She couldn't stand the silence.

Then it started. Mel's phone rang first. She jumped to answer it. 'Beech Hill Rescue Centre ... yes, that's right ... what kind of pet are you looking for? A cat ... the little black one on the telly?'

Carly gave a deep sigh. 'That's Jet,' she whispered to Hoody. The black kitten had come across as lively and full of fun.

'That's great,' Hoody answered, allowing himself a brief grin.

' . . . Could you give me your name and telephone number?' Bupinda was saying at the end of her first call. 'Yes, I'll make a note of that. You'd like one of the Border collie pups? The one with the black ears and white nose. Yes, I've got that, thanks. We're telling everyone to come and see the animals between ten and twelve tomorrow morning. OK, see you then.' She put the phone down and gave Carly a thumbs-up sign.

'Happy now?' her dad asked. Both phones were ringing without a gap.

' . . . Yes, the silver-grey kitten. I've got that. I'll put you on the list and we'll get back to you.'

' . . . OK, you'd like a Labrador pup. You don't mind which one? Fine. We'd like you to come in and look at them. Is that all right?'

Mel and Bupinda worked as fast as they could.

Carly nodded. 'It's fantastic!'

'Guess what, I've even had a call about the new

cruelty case that Steve brought in. A lady is offering him a home out in the country as soon as he's better!' Mel was loving every minute, jotting down notes and taking more calls.

'What about you, Hoody? Aren't you pleased?' Paul Grey asked.

'Ask me later,' came the short answer. Hoody couldn't stay still. He sat down on a bench, then stood up, flicked through the leaflets in the rack, pretended to read a poster on the wall.

'What's up? Isn't this what you and Carly wanted?'

'Course.'

'Well then?'

'It's great for Jet and the others. I'm not saying it isn't . . .' Hoody bit his lip, then blurted out the problem. 'But no one's rung up for Vinny yet, have they? And he's the one who needs a home most!'

10

The phone calls kept coming in right through the evening. But none were about Vinny.

Jet, Diamond and Ruby had people queuing up to take them home. Bella's pups could have been sold six times over. The Border collies were almost as popular.

'It's the "aah!" factor,' Liz told Hoody and Carly. 'Everyone goes gooey over a sweet little kitten or puppy and wants to take it home. But we'll still have to be careful that we get the right sort of owner; not someone who'll lose interest

118

as soon as the animal grows up.'

Nevertheless, they were sure that the future of the kittens and puppies was secure.

'Why doesn't anybody want Vinny?' Hoody demanded, angry with all the stupid people who fell for sweet little balls of fur without recognising the mongrel dog's worth. 'He'd make a brilliant pet, if only they knew it!'

Afraid that he was going to storm out of the Centre, Carly tried to calm him down. 'Wait and see,' she urged. 'People are still ringing up. Maybe, sooner or later, one will be about Vinny.'

'They'd better hurry up,' Hoody grumbled. He took Carly to one side. 'When are they actually going to . . . ? I mean, when are they meant to . . . ?'

'Put Vinny to sleep?' Paul Grey overheard. He could see how much Vinny meant to Hoody. 'It's scheduled for later tonight,' he said as gently as possible.

'But we could put it off!' Carly begged. 'Give him another twenty-four hours!'

'I don't usually mess about with this sort of deadline,' he explained. 'No one likes doing it, but in one way it's as well to get it over and done with.'

'Oh no!' Normally Carly would have accepted his decision, but tonight was different. Vinny was different! 'Just this once, Dad! Give someone a chance to ring up and give him a home, please! Maybe they saw the programme and haven't got round to it yet!' The phone calls were still coming through; more of a trickle now, it was true, but people were offering. Names were being added to the list.

'I agree this is an unusual situation,' Paul Grey said quietly. He noticed Liz listening in on their conversation. 'What do you think?'

Liz considered the problem from all angles. Carly and Hoody felt the silence gape wide open. They hung on to their belief that Vinny would eventually find an owner.

'Put it off until tomorrow,' Liz said at last.

Twenty-four more hours for Vinny, Hoody and Carly.

'Who's a star?' Harmony Brown had come in a taxi later that evening to collect Brandy. Her stay in hospital had gone well, the minor operation on her eyes had been successful.

When Carly brought Brandy in from the kennels, the dog was overjoyed to see her. He'd heard her voice in reception and jumped up at the kennel door in delight. Now he pushed his nose against her hand and clamoured for attention.

'I hear you were on television!' Harmony beamed down at him. 'I hope you were a good boy!'

'He was perfect,' Carly told her. 'We groomed him to look really smart, and he behaved like a model dog.'

'I'm so proud!' Harmony fastened Brandy's harness and took hold of the handle. 'And did the programme help you to find homes for all your abandoned animals?'

'Nearly all.' All except for Vinny. She glanced at Hoody, who sat on the bench by the window, watching the sky grow dark.

'You must be very pleased.' The blind woman smiled and turned to go. 'My taxi's waiting. I want to thank you for taking such good care of

Brandy. Now I won't be afraid to leave him again. It's a terrific weight off my mind.'

Carly said goodbye to the guide dog and watched him lead his mistress to the door. Back in harness, he was calm and obedient. Harmony stepped confidently after him, head up, listening hard, trusting Brandy to be her eyes.

'It's OK for some,' Hoody muttered after they'd gone. Worrying about Vinny was making him sulky and angry.

The phone calls had trickled away to nothing. Mel and Bupinda had packed up and gone home. Outside, the orange streetlamps had come on. In a few minutes it would be completely dark.

'Carly, can you come up and give me a hand?' Paul Grey called down from the first floor. 'I'm a bit concerned about the tortoiseshell kitten. I need you to hold her while I examine her.'

'I'd better go,' Carly told Hoody. 'Why don't you go home and get something to eat?'

'I'm not hungry. Anyway, there might be a phone call.'

'Not now.' She didn't think anyone would ring

up about Vinny tonight. 'Maybe tomorrow. Come back then.'

He got up, looking lost and troubled. 'I really thought someone would ring up for him!'

She nodded. 'Me too.' She didn't know what to say to make him feel better. 'Listen, how early can you get here in the morning?'

'Early as you want. Why?'

'I thought we could go down to the allotments on King Edward's Road.'

'To check out this story about the cats?'

'If you still want to.' She headed for the stairs, but paused to wait for his answer. 'We might find out more about who dumped them.'

Hoody slouched towards the door, hands in his pockets. 'If you like. I don't know, I might be busy.'

Carly turned away impatiently. 'Please yourself.' It wasn't her fault that Vinny was still homeless. Why take it out on her? She went upstairs two at a time, hardly caring whether or not Hoody decided to set foot inside Beech Hill ever again.

*

'Pneumonia,' Paul Grey decided as he listened to Ruby's chest. He'd been keeping an eye on her all through the night, and now he was quite sure that the bronchitis had turned into full-blown pneumonia.

'Is she strong enough to fight it?' Carly wanted to know. Holding the kitten in one hand, she thought Ruby seemed frail and tiny.

'We'll have to wait and see. I've given her another dose of antibiotics. If she'd still been living rough, without proper shelter and care, there's no doubt about it: she would definitely have died. At least in here she's in with a chance.'

'But pneumonia!' Carly protested. Ruby fought for breath. She refused to feed. While Jet and Diamond got stronger by the hour, she lay miserable and listless.

'Yes. She needs more fluids, so I'm going to put her on a drip. You can help me if you like.'

They got to work, attaching a tube to the needle which Paul inserted under Ruby's skin. Carly taped the needle in place while her dad hooked the tube into a clear carton containing the salt solution that their sick patient needed.

Then Carly carried Ruby, complete with drip attachment, to the intensive care unit, where she would be warm and quiet. Someone would check her every few minutes. She would receive the very best care.

'What now?' Paul Grey was getting ready for the rush of visitors. It was half past nine. At ten o'clock the keen volunteers who'd put their names on the list for a pet would begin to arrive. 'Time for breakfast?'

Carly shook her head. 'I'm not hungry, thanks.' She wiped down the treatment table which they'd used for Ruby.

'Try not to worry.' He gave her a hug. 'I take it Hoody didn't show up this morning?'

'No. Anyway, I thought I'd take Vinny for a walk instead.' She told him she would be gone for a couple of hours. 'I'd rather be out of the way when the crowd gets here,' she explained.

Somehow it was worse, knowing that there were so many happy endings about to happen. As she collected Vinny from the kennels and took him through reception, Bupinda was telling Liz about other offers of help.

'We've had dozens of donations through the post this morning,' she said excitedly. 'One cheque was for a hundred pounds!'

'It's wonderful what people will give,' Liz agreed. 'And you know the TV company who made the film? I just heard that they're going to lead a campaign to raise money to fund a new intensive care unit for us!'

'That's worth thousands!' Bupinda could hardly believe their luck.

That's the good news, Carly thought, slipping into Hoody's way of seeing things. *Now for the bad news*. She sidled up to the desk to read Bupinda's list.

'What are you looking for?' the receptionist asked, ready to help. She was smiling and bustling about, ready for the rush.

'An owner for Vinny. Has anyone offered?'

'Afraid not. Sorry, Carly. I know it's tough.'

She promised to do her best if anyone else rang up.

'I didn't expect anyone to; not really.' By now Carly had almost given up. *Let's face it*, she said to herself as she took Vinny out for what would probably be his final walk, *if anyone who saw the programme had wanted him, they would have rung up before now.* She walked aimlessly up the street towards the main road, hardly noticing the traffic.

Saturday morning, busy with shoppers. A boy delivering newspapers cycled by. The fruit stall outside Hillman's was piled high with apples, oranges and grapefruit. Carly and Vinny crossed the main road and took a sidestreet. Almost without thinking, she looked up at the sign and saw that they were on King Edward's Road.

Now that they were here, she might as well carry on down to the allotments. Not that she expected to find out much, but she might see the garden shed where Daisy had lived and given birth to her kittens, and perhaps there would be a clue; someone who knew exactly what had happened.

'Hey!' a voice called.

Carly stood with Vinny at the allotment fence. It was a dull, grey morning with a light drizzle falling. She thought at first that the man was shouting at her.

'Come out of there!' He yelled at someone else. 'That's private property!'

She saw the man waving his arms and striding up the path. A shed door was swinging open and a skinny figure in jeans and trainers came out.

'What are you up to? If you don't clear off, I'll call the police!' The angry man stormed up to Hoody. 'Come on, what are you nosing around inside my shed for?' He wore heavy gardening boots and an old anorak.

'Looking for a cat,' Hoody said. He hadn't seen Carly and Vinny. 'I heard there was one living here.'

'Not any more. It had kittens so I cleared them out. I can't stand the nasty, smelly things.'

Here was the solution to the mystery of Daisy: a small man in an anorak who wasn't even embarrassed about what he'd done. A gardener who cared more about his cabbages than about living creatures. Carly stood speechless.

Hoody broke the news about what had happened to Daisy and her three kittens after he'd dumped them on the dual carriageway.

'What do you want me to do about it?' the man

said, shrugging it off. 'I never wanted the cat in my shed in the first place. I just wish I'd got rid of it before it had kittens.'

It was useless to argue. Hoody turned away and for the first time spotted Carly and Vinny. For a moment he made as if to go off in the opposite direction, then he changed his mind and came across.

'Did you hear that?' he asked. By now the man was banging about inside his shed. 'He doesn't even care!'

Carly sighed. 'At least we know what happened.'

'Will you take him to court?'

Hoody had taken hold of Vinny's lead and they'd begun to walk together back up the street. 'I'll tell Steve and see what he says.'

In a way she didn't see the point. The culprit was just a little man who loved gardening and didn't like cats messing up his vegetable patch. When she saw him in the flesh, she didn't feel as angry as she'd expected. 'Steve will probably come down here and ask him to get in touch with Beech Hill if it happens again.'

'It'll save him the trouble of having to dump them,' Hoody agreed. He gave a twisted smile. 'Any news on Vinny?'

'I thought you didn't care any more.' They reached the main road and waited to cross.

'I never said that,' he protested. He stroked Vinny's head as the dog sat on the kerb.

'No, sorry.' Obviously Hoody cared. It was because of him that they'd finally discovered the truth about Daisy. He, more than anyone else, cared about waifs and strays. 'There was no news last night or earlier this morning, but come on, let's go back and see what's happening now.'

The pedestrian crossing flashed green and they set off, Vinny pulling ahead now, heading for home.

'Look at the queue!' Carly said. Beech Hill came into sight. People were standing outside the door, taking their turn to go in and view the kennels.

Vinny charged on regardless.

'Watch where you're going,' someone at the back of the queue complained to Hoody. 'You nearly knocked me over. Can't you do something to control that dog?'

Carly sighed. This was not the way for Vinny to win new friends. He barged through the crowd to more complaints.

'Take your turn,' a woman insisted. 'We were here first.'

'I don't like the look of that dog,' a man muttered. 'He looks a bit vicious to me.'

But at last they were inside reception, where it was at least warm and dry. People at the desk were signing forms and taking leaflets, while others queued patiently.

'Carly, Hoody, there you are!' Paul Grey waved and called them across.

'How's Ruby?' she asked.

'Holding her own. But I didn't want to talk to you about that. It's Vinny.'

Carly swallowed hard. She saw Hoody grip more tightly on the lead. Vinny looked up at the mention of his name.

'Did someone ring?' she breathed. *Please let the answer be yes*!

'Not exactly.' Paul cleared his throat. 'But

there's been a development . . .'

A young woman turned from the counter to face them. She was tall and thin, with short brown hair and a row of gold studs in each ear.

'Zoe?' Hoody's mouth dropped open. 'What are you doing here?'

'Looking for you,' his sister said. 'I thought I might find you here.'

'Why, what's wrong?' Hoody held on to Vinny's lead, ready for trouble.

'Nothing's wrong, except you won't stay in one place long enough for me to have a word with you!'

Carly glanced at her dad. He was by the desk, flicking through some papers with a half-smile on his face.

'You come in late last night and shoot straight off to your room. You're up at the crack of dawn and out of the house before I'm even awake.' Zoe was determined to pin him down now, though. She caught hold of his jacket sleeve and went on.

'Listen, we saw you on the telly last night. Dean and me were having our tea. Dean was the one who spotted you. "Isn't that your Hoody?"

he said. You could've knocked me down. Anyway, we were dead proud. Dean went out and told all his mates about what you were doing to help those poor animals.'

Carly saw Hoody blush bright red. He stooped to pat Vinny, pretending he didn't care if they were proud of him or not.

'You know what Dean's like,' Zoe went on in a rush, still tugging at Hoody's jacket. 'You know how he always says he hates dogs?'

Hoody jerked upright, looked his sister straight in the face. 'So?'

'Well, to cut a long story short, when he saw you on the telly, and how good you were with this dog, he had a change of heart. That's what I've been trying to tell you since last night. Dean says you can bring Vinny home to our house!'

It was Sunday morning. The queues had gone, and every single abandoned animal at Beech Hill had been promised a home. Carly sat at a sunny living-room window, looking out over the park. She nursed Ruby on her lap, while her dad read the weekend papers.

'Don't spoil that kitten!' he warned, looking over the top of his magazine. It was only a couple of hours since he'd declared her out of danger and taken her off the drip. 'She'll get so used to being doted on by you that she won't want to leave!' He disappeared again behind the colour supplement.

'Da-ad!' Carly began. He'd put an unbelievable thought into her head. 'You know that rule we have about not adopting any animals ourselves . . . ?' It was a rule they'd stuck to ever since she could remember.

'Hmm.'

'Well, Ruby is really special, isn't she? And I was wondering . . . if just for once we could break the rule?' Too much to hope for, probably. She steeled herself to hear the answer, 'No'.

'Yes,' Paul Grey said, putting down his paper and grinning broadly. 'I wondered when you'd finally get round to asking! Ruby can stay with us!'

'Oh, thanks, Dad!' She put Ruby down and went to put her arms around him. She hugged him until he said he was out of breath.

'Well, rules are made to be broken once in a while!' He shuffled off to make coffee, whistling as he went.

Ruby the orphan. Ruby the kitten who'd been left to die. And now Ruby the Beech Hill cat. It was Carly's dream come true.

She picked her up and showed her round the living room. 'This is my dad's chair and these are his slippers. This is the table where I do my homework. And this is the view out of the window.'

Together they looked down on to the park. They could see the pond with the Canada geese, the football pitches, the grassy slope where people walked their dogs. They could see a boy throwing a sturdy stick for a mongrel. The stick flew through the air, the dog barked and gave chase.

'And that's Hoody and his dog, Vinny,' Carly told Ruby. 'I expect you'll be seeing a whole lot more of *them* in future!'

Another Hodder Children's book

Look out for the third book in this series . . .

ANIMAL
ALERT

KILLER ON THE LOOSE

City life moves fast, but so do the staff at Beech Hill Rescue Centre – if there's an animal in danger, they're first on the scene!

Wild rumours are flying around Beech Hill. A spate of violent attacks has left a Jack Russell with a torn face and a cat fatally injured.

A stray German shepherd has been spotted in the park and locals are sure he's to blame. They want him caught and put down – as soon as possible!

Carly's not convinced the dog's a killer – but will she have time to prove it . . . ?

ANIMAL ALERT SERIES
Jenny Oldfield

All Hodder Children's books are available at your local bookshop or newsagent, or can be ordered direct from the publisher. Just tick the titles you want and fill in the form below. Prices and availability subject to change without notice.

Hodder Children's Books, Cash Sales Department, Bookpoint, 39 Milton Park, Abingdon, OXON, OX14 4TD, UK. If you have a credit card you may order by telephone – (01235) 831700.

Please enclose a cheque or postal order made payable to Bookpoint Ltd to the value of the cover price and allow the following for postage and packing:
UK & BFPO – £1.00 for the first book, 50p for the second book, and 30p for each additional book ordered up to a maximum charge of £3.00.
OVERSEAS & EIRE – £2.00 for the first book, £1.00 for the second book, and 50p for each additional book.

Name ....

Address...

....

....

If you would prefer to pay by credit card, please complete:
Please debit my Visa/Access/Diner's Card/American Express (delete as applicable) card no:

Signature ....

Expiry Date ....

If you would like to receive the Jenny Oldfield newsletter, please either send an A5 stamped addressed envelope to the following address, or ask at your local bookshop:

Jenny Oldfield Newsletter
Marketing Department
Hodder Children's Books
338 Euston Road
London NW1 3BH